Caught
–in the–
Rebel Camp

Trailblazer Books

HISTORIC CHARACTERS	TITLE
Gladys Aylward	Flight of the Fugitives
Mary McLeod Bethune	Defeat of the Ghost Riders
William & Catherine Booth	Kidnapped by River Rats
Charles Loring Brace	Roundup of the Street Rovers
William Bradford	The Mayflower Secret
John Bunyan	Traitor in the Tower
Amy Carmichael	The Hidden Jewel
Peter Cartwright	Abandoned on the Wild Frontier
Maude Cary	Risking the Forbidden Game
George Washington Carver	The Forty-Acre Swindle
Frederick Douglass	Caught in the Rebel Camp
Elizabeth Fry	The Thieves of Tyburn Square
Chief Spokane Garry	Exiled to the Red River
Barbrooke Grubb	Ambushed in Jaguar Swamp
Jonathan & Rosalind Goforth	Mask of the Wolf Boy
Sheldon Jackson	The Gold Miners' Rescue
Adoniram & Ann Judson	Imprisoned in the Golden City
Festo Kivengere	Assassins in the Cathedral
David Livingstone	Escape From the Slave Traders
Martin Luther	Spy for the Night Riders
Dwight L. Moody	Danger on the Flying Trapeze
Lottie Moon	Drawn by a China Moon
Samuel Morris	Quest for the Lost Prince
George Müller	The Bandit of Ashley Downs
John Newton	The Runaway's Revenge
Florence Nightingale	The Drummer Boy's Battle
John G. Paton	Sinking the Dayspring
William Penn	Hostage on the Nighthawk
Joy Ridderhof	Race for the Record
Nate Saint	The Fate of the Yellow Woodbee
Rómulo Sauñe	Blinded by the Shining Path
William Seymour	Journey to the End of the Earth
Menno Simons	The Betrayer's Fortune
Mary Slessor	Trial by Poison
Hudson Taylor	Shanghaied to China
Harriet Tubman	Listen for the Whippoorwill
William Tyndale	The Queen's Smuggler
John Wesley	The Chimney Sweep's Ransom
Marcus & Narcissa Whitman	Attack in the Rye Grass
David Zeisberger	The Warrior's Challenge

Caught
–in the–
Rebel Camp

Dave & Neta Jackson

Illustrated by Anne Gavitt

CASTLE
ROCK
CREATIVE
Evanston, Illinois 60202

Published by Castle Rock Creative, Inc.
Evanston, Illinois 60202

Previously published by
Bethany House, a division of
Baker Publishing Group

Unless otherwise noted, all Scripture quotations are from the King James Version of the Bible

Inside illustrations by Anne Gavitt
Cover illustration by Catherine Reishus McLaughlin

ISBN: 978-0-9982107-0-4

Printed in the United States of America

For a complete listing of
books by Dave and Neta Jackson visit
www.daveneta.com
www.trailblazerbooks.com

The basic elements of Frederick Douglass's story—born into slavery, self-educated, conversion at age thirteen, escape at age twenty and marriage to Anna, rising to become a powerful and eloquent speaker for the abolition of slavery, raising his family on St. Paul Road on the outskirts of Rochester, New York—are all true. Two of his sons—Lewis and Charles—joined the Fifty-Fourth Massachusetts Infantry Volunteers, and Sergeant Major Lewis Douglass was beside Colonel Robert Shaw, the commander of the Fifty-Fourth, when Shaw led the charge and was killed at Fort Wagner.

Thomas Sims was indeed a runaway slave who was captured in Boston and returned to slavery under the Fugitive Slave Law; twelve years later he was in the crowd as a free man when the Fifty-Fourth marched through Boston to the cheers of its citizens.

However, Danny Sims and his relationship to "Uncle Thomas" and the Douglasses is entirely fictional. However, oys too young to fight as soldiers did serve as drummer boys, runners, orderlies, and grooms.

The lost horse, Danny's getting "caught" in Fort Wagner, and his role in returning Shaw's horse are fiction. However, Colonel Shaw loved fine horses, and one source says he requested his favorite horse be sent back to his wife if anything happened to him.

Special thanks to Private Riley Ewen—a young teen Civil War re-enactor who "runs powder" for the First Chicago Light Artillary, Battery B, and also serves with the First Michigan Engineers, Company E —for his expert factual consultation.

CONTENTS

Chapter 1

Race by the River
September 1862, Rochester, New York

Hugging the round sides of the big bay with his knees, Danny Sims leaned back slightly to keep his seat as the horse picked its way down the trail to the river below. Maybe he should have put on the saddle today... but the fourteen-year-old loved the feel of the bay's muscles moving smoothly beneath his legs, with only the reins and a handful of coarse black mane to keep him topside.

At the bottom of the trail, a narrow rocky beach ran beside the Genesee River flowing south out of Lake Ontario a few miles to the north, spilling over the Upper Falls a mile behind him downstream, and churning the massive water wheels of the flour mills that gave Rochester, New York, its nickname of "Flour City." But here, above the falls, the river was smooth and deep, captured between the rocky hillsides on either side. Danny eased his grip on the reins and let the horse drink.

The river and its trails was one of Danny's favorite haunts, especially on horseback. He sometimes pretended he was a Seneca Indian brave, scouting for new game or spying on the white trappers who'd used the inlet to the river from the Big Lake. But mostly he figured he was one of the luckiest boys alive, getting paid ten cents a day to take care of Frederick Douglass's carriage horses. From time to time he got jobs from some of the other country homes along St. Paul Road, just a few miles outside of Rochester—"country gentlemen" who traveled to New York on business and wanted a boy to exercise their horses for a week.

Danny couldn't remember a time when he wasn't crazy about horses. Seemed like all he'd ever wanted to do, from the time he could pull himself up on his grammy's skirts, was to sit on the backs of those magnificent beasts. Forget walking. Forget stumbling and falling. On a horse, he was fleet as a white-tailed buck. Brave as a Seneca warrior. King of the world.

The bay lifted its head with a *whoosh*, muzzle wet and dripping, and pricked its ears toward the road above. Danny cocked his head. He couldn't hear anything. "C'mon, Wendell. Let's go on back. William gonna be kickin' a fine fuss if I don' get some hay in that manger soon." Danny chuckled silently in his belly, thinking about "Wendell" and "William" as the pair headed back up the trail to the road. He wondered if the two famous abolitionists—Wendell Phillips and William Garrison—knew about their four-legged namesakes.

Danny had to hold tight to Wendell's mane to keep from sliding off the bay's bare rump as the pair scrambled back up the steep trail to St. Paul Road above. As they emerged from the scrub bushes at the top, Danny suddenly pulled up short.

Two white boys stood on the other side of the road, pointing a pair of muzzle-loaders right between Wendell's ears.

"Man!" said the taller of the two, slowly lowering his rifle. "Just a darkie and a nag." He spit in disgust. "We thought you was an eight-point buck coming up that draw."

"What you doin' down there anyway, huh?" said the other. "Nobody *rides* those steep trails down to the river."

Danny's heart was starting to slow down after his shock. He shrugged, pretending indifference. "Guess I ain't nobody, then, 'cause Wendell and me rides these trails all the time." He sucked air through his teeth. "And this ain't no nag. Belongs to Frederick Douglass."

The boys snickered. Both were older than Danny—maybe sixteen, seventeen. He couldn't recall seeing them before, and that made him nervous.

"So what?" said the tall one. "Still a nag." He was grinning beneath a hank of limp brown hair under a wool cap. "Now, if you want to ride a real horse, lookee there." He jerked his free thumb toward a clump of trees behind his shoulder. For the first time Danny saw two riding horses tied to the low branches of a northern pine just off the road.

Danny gave the horses a quick once-over with a practiced eye. One was a long-legged gray, the other a red roan. Nice-looking horses. But the gray had weak hindquarters, and the roan had a dull look about the eyes. He pursed his lips. Call Wendell a nag, would they?

"Not bad," he said carelessly. He kicked Wendell into the middle of the road. "But I bet my horse can beat both of yours in a race."

The older boys stared at Danny, then hooted with laughter. "Hear that, Sam?" said the tall one. "This young 'un is challenging us to a race."

"He got it, then," said the one called Sam. "C'mon, Tom! He's asking to get his nag licked."

Danny could have bitten his tongue the moment he spoke his challenge. What would Mr. Douglass think about racing his carriage horse? Wendell was a good horse, no doubt about it. But racing? Danny had never pushed him to the limit. But the bay had one annoying habit—a habit that might work in Danny's favor: stable fever. Once Wendell thought he was heading for home...

Tom and Sam rode up just then on the gray and the roan, their hunting rifles back at the clump of trees. Danny pointed north, away from Rochester, away from Wendell's stable. "There's a bend in the road, 'bout half a mile that way. Old stump by the road beyond the bend. Circle the stump and come back here. First horse to cross..." He stopped. Cross what? He wasn't about to get down to draw a line in the dirt road.

"First one to cross my hat," smirked Tom, pulling the wool cap off his head and tossing it to the ground.

It was agreed. The three boys lined up their horses behind the cap in the road, facing north. "On the count of three, then," said Danny. "One... two..."

Wendell wasn't happy with heading north instead of heading home. He wasn't happy hobnobbing with two strange horses instead of William, his carriage mate. Danny was counting on Wendell's unhappiness. If he could only get him to that stump...

"Three!"

With a whoop and a holler, Tom and Sam kicked their horses into a gallop. Startled, Wendell sprang to life and ran after the other two. Danny gripped tighter with his knees, a rein in either hand low on the horse's neck. The gray and the roan were pulling ahead, but Danny wasn't worried... not if he could keep Wendell within a length or two. With smug satisfaction, he noticed that the gray's hind legs splayed out in awkward fashion as he ran. That horse wouldn't be keeping up the pace long. The roan mare, now... what would she do? Danny was betting that the dull-eyed mare didn't have the heart for a real race.

Tom and Sam were shouting in glee and leering over their shoulders at Danny, still eating dust in their wake. But as the trio of horses rounded the bend and the stump loomed on their right, Danny gripped his knees tighter to Wendell's bare sides and leaned low over his neck. "Easy now, boy. Once

around the stump... just like we always do... and you're on your way home."

Danny kicked Wendell's left side, sending his mount shooting right. Out of the corner of his eye, he saw the gray overshoot the stump and heard Tom hollering, "Turn! Turn! You good-for-nothing bag o' bones!" With the gray running straight and Wendell splitting right, the roan seemed confused. Who to follow?

Danny didn't wait. This was his chance. "Home! Home!" he hissed, lying low over Wendell's neck, tasting clumps of black mane in his mouth. Beneath his legs, he felt a surge of power as Wendell regained the road. "Home!" he yelled. A twinge of guilt tickled his conscience. Yes, they were headed "home," but no way was he going to let Wendell run all the way back to the Douglass home—not just yet.

In a few minutes, it was all over. With thundering hooves, Wendell sailed past the cap in the road, the gray and the roan trailing five or six lengths behind. Hauling on the reins with all his might, Danny yelled, "Whoa! Whoa!" But Wendell would have none of it. He was heading for home.

Finally running Wendell off the road and turning him in a wide circle, Danny trotted back to where Tom and Sam sat their wheezing horses, glaring at him. Danny just smiled. "Beat ya. Fair and square."

Tom slid off the gray and snatched up his cap. "All right. So your nag can run. How 'bout you? Can you run?"

Danny's throat constricted, cutting off his air.

15

"Cat got your tongue, boy?" Tom leered. "I'm challenging you to a foot race. Right here. Right now."

Now Danny's heart was pounding. His neck veins throbbed. Licking his dry lips, he tried to find his voice. "Can't," he squeaked. "Gotta get this horse back to the Douglass place. Maybe 'nother time."

Tom's eyes narrowed. "Not another time. Now! We did your challenge—only fair for you to do ours."

"Sorry," Danny mumbled, pulling on the reins to turn Wendell around. "Gotta go."

"I—said—now!" With a swift movement, the tall boy grabbed Danny's pant leg and pulled. Taken off balance as Wendell moved the other way, Danny tumbled to the ground and hit the dust. He scrambled to his feet, still holding on to the reins, running in little hop-steps as Wendell danced away.

Tom and Sam were staring at Danny's bare feet. Then they started to laugh. "Why, you got yourself a clubfoot, there, boy. Ha, ha, ha!" Danny's face flamed with heat as the two white boys doubled over, pointing at his right foot. "Ho! Ho! You're nothin' but a cripple. Can't even walk straight, much less run. Ho! Ho! Ho!"

Gritting his teeth, Danny grasped two handfuls of black mane and hauled himself onto Wendell's back. It took all his willpower to hold back the words he would have liked to spit back in their leering faces. But it wouldn't do any good—just lead to a fight. And two to one weren't odds in his favor.

To his chagrin, the two boys followed twenty yards behind him as he headed south on St. Paul Road—just close enough for him to hear their taunting laughter. Danny held Wendell to a slow trot, trying to cool him down before reaching the lane leading up to the Douglasses' rambling ten-room house. As he turned into the lane, he could hear the parting taunts behind his back as the two boys rode past: "Cripple! Turtle!"

Tears stung Danny's eyes as he slid off Wendell's bare back at the stable. He brushed them away angrily with the back of his hand and busied himself rubbing down the sweating horse with a fistful of straw, forking fresh hay into the mangers for both Wendell and William, and hauling water from the well for their water buckets. His clubfoot gave him an awkward gait, but he prided himself on doing his chores quickly.

Maybe he couldn't run a footrace, but he was no turtle.

Done at last with his stable chores, Danny splashed his face with well water and headed for the kitchen door. Mrs. Douglass always had something for him to eat before he set out for home. No one was in the kitchen, but he could hear voices at the front end of the house. Passing through the dining room, he saw a table set with the Douglasses' good Blue Willow china. His spirits picked up, remembering he and his Uncle Thomas had been invited to stay for supper tonight at the Douglass home. Some kind of anniversary; he couldn't remember what for. His stomach growled in happy expectation. Uncle Thomas was all right—but he couldn't cook like Anna Douglass!

Then the voices at the front end of the house became clearer—Frederick Douglass, for sure. No mis-
taking that booming voice. And... must be Lewis, the
Douglasses' oldest son. Even from the dining room,
Danny couldn't help but hear the rising argument.

"Panama?" boomed the older Douglass. "We're in
the middle of a Civil War in this country! Slavery's
got its head on the chopping block, and you want to
run away to *Panama*?"

Chapter 2

Double Anniversary

PANAMA? DANNY WRACKED HIS BRAIN, trying to remember his geography lessons. Where in the world was Panama?

Curious, he tiptoed through the dining room and into the sitting room. Just off the sitting room, the door of Mr. Douglass's study was standing wide open. Not wanting to appear to be actually eavesdropping—the door *was* wide open, after all— Danny sat down on a long sofa in the sitting room adjacent to the study. Through the open doorway, he could see Mr. Douglass standing with his back to his large desk, facing someone whom Danny could not see from the sofa.

"Not running away, Father!" Definitely Lewis's voice. "I just don't have the same hope you do that this... this unholy brawl between North and South is going to dislodge slavery in this country—or give us citizenship, even if it did. You saw what happened after Mr. Lincoln was elected. South Carolina had a tantrum, and what did the government do? Fell all over itself trying to wheedle them back into the Union and keep any other slave states from falling out. Huh! Even *after* they fired on Fort Sumter, Secretary Seward promised, 'The status of no class of people will be changed by the rebellion.' Might as well have said black folks *still* goin' to be at the bottom of the heap no matter who wins."

Danny watched out of the corner of his eye as the older man frowned, thumbs in the small pockets of his waistcoat. Frederick Douglass was an imposing figure. A big bush of graying hair stood out on the sides of his face, framing a neatly trimmed mustache and beard. His skin was a medium brown, a visible heritage from his slave mother and white father. His build was solid, wide at the shoulders, dressed as usual in a tailored suit, white collar, and short, knotted tie.

He spoke. No, rumbled. "Lewis! How can you even *think* of joining the movement to colonize American blacks to other countries—you, *my* son?" He snorted. "Especially after I publicly rebuked the president last month for supporting colonization."

Twenty-two-year-old Lewis Douglass wandered into Danny's view, suit coat akimbo, waving his arms. "That's just it, Father! Even Lincoln—the great 'friend of freedom,' I think you called him—thinks colonization is the solution to the race problems in this country. I know *I* don't want to live in a country where I can't even vote, can't help determine my own destiny. Can't even fight in this bloody war that's supposed to be about *our* freedom!"

The frown on Mr. Douglass's brow deepened. "Can't you wait to make your decision, Lewis? At least until the war is over. I don't believe the Union army can long survive without calling on free blacks who want to fight for their country. The North may think this war is only about preserving the Union, but slavery is at the heart of this rebellion and will need to be reckoned with."

"I don't know, Father." Lewis's voice was almost a groan. "Are any of us safe? Even you were an outlaw until you bought your freedom." His tone grew mocking. "My father—the great abolitionist, Frederick Douglass!—speaking all over Europe, and you couldn't even come back to America till you paid that miserable Thomas Auld for your freedom—which he stole from you in the first place!"

Frederick Douglass did not reply.

"And don't forget Danny's uncle!" Danny sat bolt upright on the sofa at hearing his name. "Not twelve years ago, Thomas Sims was hunted down like an animal, dragged through the streets of Boston, thrown on a ship, and carted back to slavery... *legally*."

"I haven't forgotten Thomas Sims," Douglass said

tersely. "The Fugitive Slave Law is a curse! But he's a free man today, Lewis, largely because abolitionists took up his—"

"And now General Lee is marching into northern states!" Lewis interrupted. "They got better generals than we do! What if the South *wins* this war, Father? How long till free blacks in the north are forced into slavery, too?"

Danny had been listening so intently to father and son that he didn't even hear Anna Douglass coming until her black silk skirts swished right past him and into the study.

"Lewis!" she chirped. "I'm so glad you've come! Has anyone seen Rosetta? Or Freddie and Charles?" Almost as an afterthought, as though just remembering that she'd passed Danny on the sofa, she turned and looked back at him. "Oh, there you are, Danny. Where's that uncle of yours? My lan'! Tryin' to get this family together around the table is like chasing marbles."

Danny popped off the sofa and stood up, suddenly aware of his bare feet. Mrs. Douglass would have a fit if he came to dinner with bare feet. Where had he left his shoes?

"Now, now," Mrs. Douglass went on, turning her attention back to her husband and eldest son. "You two look entirely too serious. Whatever it is, put it aside. We have a wedding anniversary to celebrate!" Out of the corner of his eye, as he scrambled around the sitting room trying to find the hated shoes, Danny saw Anna Douglass affectionately take her husband's arm in the study. "Twenty-four years, my dear."

"And two days," Douglass teased.

"Oh, well," she huffed. "One has to celebrate when one can get this family together. Oh!" She turned. Carriage wheels could be heard coming up the lane. "That must be Rosetta now. Danny! Run out and take care of the horse!"

The dinner party was a fine affair, in Danny's opinion—even though his uncle Thomas hadn't shown up yet. Danny found his shoes in the stable where he'd tossed them before his ride with Wendell, and Mrs. Douglass passed him as "acceptable" after making him wash his face again. Freddie, age twenty, and Charles, eighteen, showed up as Rosetta, the eldest Douglass child, helped her mother carry steaming bowls and platters into the dining room. All were "dressed for dinner," which made Danny squirm a bit at his wrinkled shirt and pants that smelled like horse, but he bowed his head obediently for the blessing of the food. The prayer was lengthy, with Mr. Douglass thanking God for twenty-four years of married life and twenty-four years of freedom from wicked slavery, as well as for each member of the Douglass family who had been born into freedom. "And Lord God, we also thank you for our little Annie, who only lived to her tenth year."

The small rustlings and coughs around the table during the long prayer suddenly hushed, even as Mr.

Douglass pronounced the Amen. Danny was afraid to look up. Annie had been only two years younger than he, and she'd followed him around like an adoring pet. He still missed her terribly. How much more her family must hurt at her absence from this celebration!

But he heard Mrs. Douglass say softly, "To Annie," and the clinking of glasses as others murmured, "To Annie." Danny raised his head. The faces around the table were soft with love and memories.

"Let's eat, my dear!" boomed Mr. Douglass. He tackled the roast chicken with a big knife as bowls of black-eyed peas and rice, ears of corn, pumpkin bread, and pitchers of apple cider passed around the table. Charles and Freddie managed to put away several helpings of food with great enthusiasm, while teasing their older sister's birdlike helpings.

"Well, there *is* a war going on," Rosetta said reproachfully.

"Not eating ain't gonna help the Union army any," guffawed Charles, his mouth full. Danny agreed with *that* and decided to help himself to another serving of black-eyed peas and rice. But his chewing slowed as he realized Lewis was frowning at him.

"Where's Thomas?" Lewis said, pointing at the empty chair beside Danny.

Danny shrugged and swallowed. He was wondering himself.

"He'll be here," soothed Mrs. Douglass. "Frederick, tell the children why this is a double anniversary."

"Nonsense, Anna, they've heard the story a hundred times." Mr. Douglass was filling his plate again.

"No, you've *told* the story a hundred times at abolition meetings from New York to Philadelphia. But our children need to hear it, too."

"Yes, Papa. Tell us again."

Mr. Douglass nodded thoughtfully. "Your mother is right. For it was she who helped me escape from bondage. I was only twenty years old, but I had determined that *that year* I would be free. But I made the big mistake"—the deep-set eyes under the shaggy brows looked around the table in mock dismay—"of attending a Methodist camp meeting *without the permission* of my master, mind you. A true crime. He threatened to sell me 'down South,' and I was afraid he meant it. I was engaged to your mother, a free woman, and she sold her own featherbed so I would have enough money to buy a train ticket. An old retired sailor gave me his seaman's papers and clothes, and thus attired, I made my way from Maryland to New York City. The New York Vigilance Committee came to my aid, or I would have died right there on the streets—or been caught by bounty hunters. In a few weeks Anna joined me, and we got married September 15, 1838—a brand-new start on a brand-new life." Mr. Douglass chuckled.

"'New' all right," Anna added, rolling her eyes. "He was Frederick *Bailey* when I met him, Frederick *Johnson* when he got to New York, and we got married as *Douglass*."

Danny stared back and forth between the two ends of the table. "Why'd you choose the name Douglass, Mr. Douglass?" he piped up.

"Ah!" Frederick Douglass rose from the table and headed for his study. As if by a signal, the family pushed back their chairs and followed him. Danny eyed the last few bites of his rice and peas but went along curiously.

Joining the family in the sitting room, Mr. Douglass handed a book to Danny. "*The Lady of the Lake* by Sir Walter Scott. I'd just finished reading it the year I was twenty. I admired one of the characters, a Scottish Lord named Douglass. There you have it." He grinned hugely and sat down on the couch, eyeing his wife and patting the seat beside him.

As Anna Douglass joined him on the couch, Danny blurted, "Did you read it, too, Mrs. Douglass?"

Lewis coughed, and there was a sudden awkward silence. Mr. Douglass patted his wife's hand. "No, no... but I read it to her, young man."

Rosetta handed her father a violin case. "Play for us, Papa—like you used to when we were children and all the neighborhood came to sing."

Danny grinned. He hadn't heard Mr. Douglass play in a long time—maybe not since Annie died. But Mr. Douglass nodded. "Why not?" And he tucked the instrument under his chin.

They called out tune after tune—'Old Dan Tucker,' 'Oh Susannah,' 'Come Out de Wilderness,' 'Old Black Joe'—singing along lustily. At one point, Douglass swung into a familiar tune and Anna scolded, "Not 'John Brown's Body,' Frederick!"

Mr. Douglass winked at Danny. "No, Anna. New words. Listen." He put down the violin and began to sing in his powerful voice, "Mine eyes have seen the glory of the coming of the Lord..." Soon everyone was joining in on the chorus—"Glo-ry, glory, hallelu-jah!"

Bang! Bang! Bang! Danny jumped. So did everyone else. None of them had heard anyone approaching until the sudden banging on the front door.

Lewis strode into the hallway, his boots clomping on the wooden floor. In the sitting room, they could hear the murmur of voices in the hall; a moment later Lewis returned with a young man in his late twenties.

"Uncle Thomas!" Danny didn't realize how anxious he'd been about his uncle's strange absence from the dinner party until relief seemed to pop out of his pores.

Thomas Sims was dressed for dinner, but he was out of breath, as if he'd been riding fast. He nodded at Mrs. Douglass. "I apologize, ma'am, for being so late. But—" His eyes darted to Mr. Douglass. "—I have news."

"Speak up, man! What is it? Did Lee attack? Where?"

Danny's uncle was still breathless. "Antietam. Maryland. They're calling it a bloodbath, sir... thousands of lives lost on both sides!"

Lewis stepped forward. "Who won the battle, Mr. Sims? Lee?"

Thomas Sims shook his head. "No. They're calling it a Union victory. Lee has turned back."

"Finally!" Frederick Douglass slapped a chairback so hard Danny thought it was going to tip over. "Finally that... that pro-slavery, military incompetent, do-nothing McClellan remembered he's a Union general!"

Chapter 3

"Men of Color! To Arms!"

THE DOUGLASS FAMILY AND THOMAS SIMS huddled in the sitting room, that day's date imprinted forever on their minds: September 17, 1862. It was a turning point, at least for now... but the loss of life to both sides was staggering to contemplate. "Twelve *thousand*, Thomas?" Anna Douglass repeated, almost in shock. "In one day?"

"That's what they're saying. Plus twice that wounded or missing." The young man put his head in his hands. "Oh, God, what a bloody day."

Even with the news that Lee had been turned back from his northward march, the faces in the Rochester house were strained.

Men and boys from Rochester had formed several Union regiments. How many families would soon get word that a father... a brother... a son had been killed, wounded, or captured at Antietam?

Frederick Douglass began pacing. "At this rate, the North is going to run out of able-bodied men to fight this war." He slammed one fist into his open hand. "If only the president would let the black men fight. It is our freedom at stake! We should be allowed to fight for it!"

Thomas Sims nodded. "That day may be coming soon, Mr. Douglass." In his dressed-for-dinner clothes, twenty-nine-year-old Thomas looked the picture of a young northern gentleman. But Danny had seen the scars on his back. "I have more news: President Lincoln is drafting the Emancipation Proclamation to be announced in a few days—to go into effect January 1."

Douglass stopped pacing. "How far does it go?"

"It will free the slaves in all the rebelling states."

"And the border slave states?"

"Not yet. The president is saying he can't afford to alienate them from the Union."

Lewis exploded. "See, Father? Will an emancipation proclamation free *your* family back in Maryland? No! Because Maryland is still loyal to the Union. He's only punishing the rebellious states—not really freeing the slaves."

Douglass held up a hand. "I know. But..." He looked around at his gathered family, at Danny and Thomas Sims. "We must embrace every step toward freedom as good news. And mark my words... this Emancipation Proclamation will set the stage allowing free blacks to fight for the right to be U.S. citizens!"

The dinner party finally broke up, and Danny rode home behind his uncle's saddle in the crisp September night. They lived in a two-room apartment over a print shop in Rochester, where Thomas worked days and studied journalism in the evenings. The horse belonged to Thomas's employer, a white abolitionist who had taken a liking to the passionate young man who was determined to improve his mind and station in life after twenty years as a slave in the South. When Grammy died—a laundress who had kept half of Rochester clean in the old days, before the Erie Canal made it a boomtown—Thomas had taken young Danny under his wing.

Thomas was keenly interested in keeping up with news of the war, but it was slow in coming. General George McClellan was sluggish in following up on his victory at Antietam; a frustrated Lincoln told him, "If you don't want to use the army, I should like to borrow it for a while"—and replaced him in November with General Ambrose Burnside as General of the Potomac. But Burnside lost over twelve thousand men at Fredericksburg, Virginia, in December—a Union defeat.

Danny tried to be interested in the war news of

his elders—the print shop below churned out the *Rochester Evening Express,* as well as Frederick Douglass's opinion paper, *Douglass's Monthly.* But he had a more immediate fight on his hands.

Tom and Sam.

Though Danny had never laid eyes on either boy before the day of the race back in September, now it seemed they popped up wherever he went. Not that he always saw them. The first time was when he was out on St. Paul Road again, exercising William this time. Blam!—a hunting rifle went off in the bushes beside the road just as they passed, spooking William, who jumped sideways and took off running willy-nilly—but not before Danny heard high-pitched whoops and giggles from the bushes. After that, he never knew when they might show up on St. Paul Road, trailing behind him and whatever horse he was exercising, making crude comments and laughing.

It rattled Danny's nerves.

One cold day in January, Danny hobbled down the icy wooden steps that led from the second-floor apartment to the street in the hop-step, hop-step gait he'd perfected because of his clubfoot—only to see Tom and Sam lounging against a coal wagon across the street, blowing warm air on their bare hands.

"Well, well," said Tom. "If it ain't our friend Turtle."

"Yeah," Sam chimed in. "Thinks he's a big shot when he's got a horse to do his runnin'. But stand 'im on his own two feet… ha! Diff'rent story."

Danny knew he should just ignore them. *Ain't nothin' they say can change who you really is inside, Danny Sims,* his grammy used to say. *You created by God Hisself—nobody else. But it ain't worth provokin' mo' trouble on yo' head by lettin' white folks know what yo' feelin' inside—or shootin' off yo' mouth, either.* But these were just boys like himself, even if they were a year or two older, and he'd beat them

fair and square in that horse race.

Poor losers, that's what they were.

"What do you two want?" Danny asked, pausing by the corner of the print shop.

"Who, us?" Tom spread his hands innocently. "Nothin'. Just passin' the time."

"Thinkin' 'bout volunteering for the army," Sam boasted.

"You too young," Danny shot back.

Tom snorted. "No, *you* too young. An' even if you was old enough, you too black." Tom was enjoying himself. "Ain't no colored troops in the Union army— 'cept to dig ditches, maybe."

Danny's blood was boiling now. "You don't know what you talkin' 'bout. President Lincoln said the army goin' to need colored troops. It was in the newspaper."

Tom shrugged as Sam giggled. "Don't matter. No self-respectin' white regiment gonna fight with no colored troops. *That* idea gonna die in the swamp water."

"Yeah," Sam chimed in again. "And it don't matter for you no way. You too clump-footed to be any good to the army. Ain't he, Tom?"

Danny knew if he didn't walk away now, he was going to end up in a fight, and it was bad odds—two to one. He stomped into the print shop, thankful for the clattering machines that covered his entrance. Uncle Thomas was probably setting headlines somewhere in the back, but Danny kept an eye out the front window until his tormentors wandered off, pleased with themselves. Slipping outside again, he set out for the two-mile walk to the Douglass house on St. Paul Road. He'd have to walk fast to keep warm in the bitter wind that swept off of Lake Ontario—not an easy feat with his lame foot encased in the torturous leather shoes he had to wear in winter.

Both William and Wendell balked at leaving their warm stable for a ride in the bitter cold, and Danny wasn't too happy about it, either. As he rubbed the horses down afterward and mucked out their stalls, he heard a commotion in the courtyard. The stable door flew open, and Mr. Douglass led in a brown horse still harnessed to a light rig. Danny recognized the rig as the kind Old Bixby rented to businessmen coming in on the New York Central.

"Danny! Give Mr. Stearns's horse a drink." Mr. Douglass pointed at a water barrel that had been rolled inside the warm stable to keep it from freezing. "He won't be here long, so leave the horse harnessed."

Danny shrugged and fetched a bucket of water. Who was Mr. Stearns? He couldn't keep up with all the men and women who found their way to the Douglass household—from New York, Boston, all over the world, it seemed.

Mildly curious, Danny finished the stable chores and made a beeline for the Douglass kitchen, hoping for some fresh homemade bread. As he let himself into the kitchen, Rose Parker—the town girl who came three days a week to help Mrs. Douglass with laundry and cooking—looked up from the winter vegetables she was chopping. "Close that door, Danny Sims!" she scolded, dumping the vegetables into a soup pot simmering on the big cast-iron stove. "This ain't the North Pole, and I ain't a penguin."

Danny shut the door. "Don't let Mr. Douglass hear you say 'ain't,' Miss Rose—he'd send you packing back to school!" Danny liked Rose, who was only nineteen or twenty, even if she did nag him to death. The two oldest Douglass offspring were living in town now, but Freddie Jr. and Charles—apprenticed to tradesmen in Rochester during the day—still lived at home, and Rose lost no opportunities to make eyes at the two handsome young men, hoping for a potential suitor. "Um, who's in there with Mr. Douglass?"

Rose sliced the end of a fresh loaf of bread. "Man named George Stearns. From Massachusetts. What I hear is they raising a black regiment to fight. Came to ask Mr. Douglass to help."

So it was true! Danny wished he could see Tom's and Sam's faces when they heard *that*. He was on his second slice of bread when Mr. Douglass and his guest—a middle-aged white man with a long, bushy brown beard that made him look like pictures of the biblical Moses—came into the kitchen. "Oh, there you are, Danny! Get Mr. Stearns's rig, will you? Then I want you to deliver a message to Thomas at the print shop—ask if he can squeeze in an extra edition of *Douglass's Monthly*. I'll have the copy to the shop tomorrow." Douglass turned back to his guest. "Can you drop the boy off at the print shop before going back to your hotel—or do you plan to catch the eastbound train tonight?"

Stearns's beard waggled as he spoke. "I can drop off the boy. But I'm leaving tonight. I have accomplished what I came for." He held out his hand. "Thank you, Mr. Douglass. You have the gratitude of Massachusetts and Governor Andrew, as well."

Frederick Douglass grasped the man's hand in return. "Give me no thanks. My motives are entirely selfish." Douglass's eyes seemed to burn with a fire that came deep from his belly. "I tell you, Stearns, once the black man gets to wear the brass letters, 'U.S.,' and gets an eagle on his buttons and a musket on his shoulder and bullets in his pockets, there will be no power on earth that can deny he has earned the right to citizenship in the United States!"

A special edition of *Douglass's Monthly* went out on March 2, 1863, with the banner headline, "Men of Color! To Arms!" Within days, black men of every age were lining up at recruiting offices to sign up for the Fifty-Fourth Regiment of Massachusetts—the first regiment of free blacks to be trained to fight in the Civil War, not merely as laborers.

Something stirred in Danny's spirit. *Could he*—? He wanted to ask Mr. Douglass, but the Douglass household was astir. Lewis Douglass had been one of the first to sign up, Charles a short while later. Rose Parker's eyes were red and puffy when Danny came in for his bread and milk after stable chores the day he heard the news. "At least Freddie ain't signin' up," she sniffled, blowing her nose on an old rag.

"Why not?" Danny asked, dunking his bread in the hot milk. "He's two years older than Charles." *And Lewis... whatever happened to Panama?* he thought.

Rose whirled on him. "'Cause war ain't no lark, Danny Sims. Don't you know them Confederates made themselves a law sayin' any black men they capture fighting for the Union army will be hung—or sold into slavery? What if Mr. Lewis or Mr. Charles gets killed... or captured?" Her eyes filled, and tears spilled down her cheeks. "No family should lose all its sons. I 'spect it was Mr. Douglass who wouldn't let Freddie go."

The idea burned in Danny's brain. Charles Douglass was only four years older than he was, and they'd let *him* enlist. Danny was big and strong for his age; he could shoot a rifle, too. But when he brought it up to his uncle, Thomas looked at him as though Danny had suggested running for president. "Put that idea out of your head, Danny! You're only fourteen. And... and not all are meant to be soldiers. I'm sure Mr. Douglass would agree."

Danny rode Wendell hard that day, the breath of both horse and boy spurting in white puffs like a New York Central steam engine as the horse's hooves pounded on the frozen road. Uncle Thomas might just as well have blurted out the real reason he wasn't "meant to be" a soldier: because he was lame, a *cripple*. His people were going off to war to fight for their very existence as free men. But not Danny. He wasn't good enough.

Wendell's hoofbeats pounded in his ears. *No good... no good...*

Chapter 4

Slacker

THERE WERE NO MORE BOISTEROUS MEALS at the Douglass household. Lewis and Charles were at Camp Meigs in Massachusetts, training under Colonel Robert Gould Shaw, son of a Boston abolitionist, and Freddie had been given a commission to recruit black troops in the Mississippi Valley. Frederick Sr. seemed pleased with this compromise. All of his sons were now in the service of the Union army, though not all in harm's way.

But Danny found it harder and harder to make the trek out to the Douglass house on St. Paul Road. He was tired of trying to avoid Tom and Sam and their shenanigans; tired of their taunts. It seemed like all the able-bodied young black men in Rochester had signed up to join the army—even his uncle was talking about becoming a war correspondent.

Everybody except Danny.

The winds blowing off Lake Ontario were heavy with spring rains, and the frozen dirt roads became rutted with mud. Walking was a chore; riding wasn't a whole lot better. "You can ride out with me," Thomas offered one gray morning in April as Danny struggled to get his left foot into the stiff leather shoe. "I need to talk to the Douglasses about something anyway."

Danny shrugged. "Okay." He hoped they didn't run into Tom and Sam. The last thing he needed was for his uncle to hear a couple of white boys making fun of him.

The ride was uneventful. Danny slid off Uncle Thomas's borrowed horse and grabbed the bridle as his uncle headed for the big, rambling house. "Come on," he said to the horse and clumped toward the stable. Hop-step. Hop-step.

Time seemed to slow down and drag as Danny plunged a pitchfork into the soiled straw in each stall and pitched clumps into a wheelbarrow. *Plunge... pitch... plunge... pitch...* Without thinking he plodded through his chores, forking clean straw into the stalls, filling the water buckets, filling the mangers with fresh hay. But he couldn't put off taking Wendell and William out for a short run forever.

Would Tom and Sam be waiting for him?

He turned onto St. Paul Road from the Douglasses' lane, riding Wendell and leading William, and headed for the old stump beyond the bend, keeping both horses to a steady trot. He was alone on the road that followed the Genesee River.

Danny thought he should feel relieved, but instead he felt disturbed. He hadn't seen those two for a couple days. Why not? And then the reason settled like a bitter taste in his mouth: they'd joined the army, just as they'd boasted they would.

Everybody except Danny.

Back at the stable, Danny swung his clubfoot and kicked an empty bucket, startling Thomas's horse, which jerked its head wildly at its tether, then kicked out in Danny's direction. He dived for a straw bale as the hooves narrowly missed his head.

"Easy, easy," Danny said, scrambling to his feet and slowly approaching the borrowed horse. The wild look in the horse's eye subsided, and it quieted under Danny's voice and hand. Danny felt like kicking himself for doing something so foolish... but he walked back to the house, hands jammed in his pockets, shoulders slumped.

Everybody but Danny.

Thomas met him at the kitchen door. "I was just coming for you, Danny. I've got something to talk about that concerns you."

Danny felt uneasy. Had someone heard him lose it in the stable? But Frederick and Anna Douglass greeted him warmly as he followed Thomas into the study. "Stand by the fireplace, Danny, and warm your fingers," Mrs. Douglass encouraged. Her knitting needles flew in and out of the navy yarn in her lap—socks and neck mufflers for Union troops.

Thomas Sims cleared his throat. Danny thought his uncle looked nervous. What was going on? "You know I've talked about being a war correspondent, Danny—a newspaper reporter covering the war. I even sent my application to several big newspapers. And I've got a job offer—from Boston."

The taste in Danny's mouth grew more bitter. Now his uncle was leaving, too.

Everybody except Danny.

"I don't know how long I'll be gone—depends on how long this war lasts. But I've asked Mr. and Mrs. Douglass if you can stay with them until I return. They have graciously said yes."

"Of course, Danny!" Anna Douglass smiled at him, even as the knitting needles continued to fly. "You are always welcome here. If Annie... if Annie were still alive, how delighted she'd be to have another brother."

Danny looked at the braided rug in front of the fireplace. Why'd she have to mention Annie? Annie *wasn't* here, and he would be alone. Everybody was off to war...

Everybody except Danny.

"This actually works out quite well, my boy," boomed Frederick Douglass. "I have gotten requests from some of our neighbors along St. Paul Road whose husbands and sons have gone off to war. They need someone to exercise their horses, who are getting a lot less use these days. It'll be easier for you if you live out here than if you have to walk all the way from town."

Danny could only stare at the rug.

"Well, Danny?" asked Uncle Thomas. "What do you say? The Douglasses are being very generous."

Danny shrugged. "It's all right, I guess. I mean, thank you."

Out of the corner of his eye, Danny saw the adults look at one another. But he didn't care. What was to care about? They'd made plans to keep him busy and keep a roof over his head while everybody else—everybody who was *good enough*—went off to war.

Everybody except Danny.

Danny didn't miss the long walks from the print shop apartment out to the Douglasses' country house. And Mrs. Douglass's cooking was a heap better than Uncle Thomas's. Mr. Douglass spent a great deal of time in his study, writing speeches, articles, and editorials about the war effort, or visiting other cities in New York, recruiting more black men for the Fifty-Fourth Massachusetts. But when the carriage wasn't needed for a trip into town or to the train station, Danny was free to ride Wendell or William over to his other stable jobs.

Danny knew he should be happy to get to work with so many different horses. All his life that had been the thing that he loved most—being around horses. He liked getting to know their different personalities, their quirks and strengths—all the things a rider or handler needed to know to bring out the best in each horse. Short of having his own horse some day—and Danny often dreamed about the steed that would one day be his—this should have been Danny's dream job.

But he didn't really care.

His clubfoot seemed to come alive, like a little demon at the end of his leg, taunting him. Growing up, he'd never been bothered much by his affliction, because it had never kept him from doing what he loved most: riding. But now his foot felt heavy, useless, mocking him as he limped around the stables on St. Paul Road: You're not good enough. You're a cripple. You're as slow as a turtle.

Mr. Douglass had to be gone for a few days in late April, attending an abolition meeting, and Mrs. Douglass had taken the team into town, so Danny had to walk to his second job that day. When he returned in late afternoon, dragging wearily up the lane, Anna Douglass met him at the kitchen door, hands on her hips.

Danny swallowed. He didn't know what he'd done, but he could tell the lady of the house was mad.

"I met Mrs. Wilson in town this morning," she announced crisply, the glare in her eyes pinning Danny to the wall. "She says she's disappointed in your work in her stable. You're slow, you waste time, you leave things undone." She pinched her mouth shut and breathed deeply through her nose, as though

searching for words. "What has gotten into you, young man? We gave you a high recommendation to our neighbors—and you reward us like this!"

Danny stared miserably at his shoes—the one straight and firm, the other bent. What did they expect from a cripple?

"Look at me when I'm talking to you!" Anna Douglass wasn't through. "No one under my roof is going to be a slacker. As long as you are eating meals at my table and sleeping in a bed under this roof, you will earn your keep—whether you're working for us or working for our neighbors. Is that understood?"

The winter mud had dried up at last; new leaves on the white oaks, maples, and hemlocks filled in the bare spots in the forest between the pines and spruce trees; and wildflowers nodded along St. Paul Road as May sprang into full bloom along the Genesee River, swollen with spring rains and Lake Ontario's melting ice.

Shedding his hated shoes, Danny tried hard to do all his stable chores faithfully. But the silence in the house, along the road, and in Rochester's diminished population of young men—white and black—sat like a stone on his heart.

But he was entirely startled when Mr. Douglass announced one evening: "Danny, pack up your clothes. We're going to Boston tomorrow."

Danny stared at the broad nose, deep-set eyes,

and fine, sculptured lips in the serious face before him, looking for a clue. None was forthcoming. That was it? Pack up your clothes, we're going to Boston?

He swallowed. "Yes, sir." But his heart sank to the bottom of his spirit, like a rock thrown into the Genesee. There could be only one reason for going to Boston: He was being returned to his uncle Thomas. The Douglasses didn't want to bother with him anymore. Maybe they'd received other complaints. He had tried to hustle, but it wasn't enough. He had let them down and they were through.

Mrs. Douglass came with them to the train station the next morning to drive the carriage back, kissed Danny with misty eyes, and waved her handkerchief as they boarded the New York Central eastbound. Mr. Douglass seemed in high spirits, which made Danny feel all the more miserable as the train jerked, huffed, and pulled out of Rochester's train station. Was he glad to be getting rid of Danny?

The train was full of passengers, mostly white, a few blacks. Two white men greeted Frederick Douglass politely by name and tipped their hats. Several others gave the pair sitting at the back of the car curious or bored expressions and looked away. Most simply ignored them, opening their newspapers, snoring in short naps, or talking about the war—always the war—with those around them.

Danny turned his face to the window. Newly planted fields, pastures, and forests rushed by. It gave him an odd feeling. He loved to ride fast, but on horseback he still felt part of the road and trees and birds and sky around and over and beneath him. But here behind a square of glass, he felt out of touch with the world out there, as if he were flipping pages in a book without reading the words.

They'd passed Syracuse and were headed for Albany, traveling in mutual silence for two to three hours, when Mr. Douglass suddenly spoke. "Danny, I have a story I want to tell you—a story about myself when I was your age, maybe a year older."

Danny looked at his companion. Sitting there side by side, they were almost the same height, though Danny had the lanky build of youth and Douglass the solid muscles and slight stoop of maturity. The boy said nothing but kept his eyes on the face beside him as the strangest story he'd ever heard unfolded....

Chapter 5

Stand Up, Young Man!

WHEN I WAS A BOY YOUR AGE," Mr. Douglass began, "I was still a 'slave for life'—part of the
'marriage property' inherited by Captain Thomas
Auld of St. Michael's, a fishing village on the eastern shore of Chesapeake Bay in Maryland. Though
I had been separated from my mother at an early
age, my one stroke of good fortune was to be sent
to Captain Auld's brother, Hugh, in Baltimore at
the age of eight to be a companion to his young son,
two-year-old Tommy. Mrs. Auld, who did not
grow up in a slave-owning family and had not
developed the slave-owner's mindset, took
a fancy to me and taught me to read...
until her husband found out about
it. The man had a fit! Was she

trying to ruin me as a slave? Slaves who could read got ideas in their heads; they began to imagine themselves equal to their masters! It was critical, said Master Hugh, that slaves be dependent upon their masters for everything, including their knowledge of the world, or there would be no end of trouble. And so my reading lessons abruptly stopped.

"Ah, but it was too late. One cannot 'unlearn' how to read. And my appetite to learn became unquenchable—all the more so because now it was forbidden. I listened as Tommy Auld was taught his lessons—and snuck his copybooks into my little loft over the kitchen, copying the alphabet letters by candlelight at night. As a member of a household in a thriving city, I quickly picked up proper English—though I had to be careful to keep my speech slow and servile. I read snatches of newspapers that were left around, though I dared not be caught. But it was from newspapers that I first learned there were people called 'abolitionists' who thought slavery was evil, and that so-called 'free states' existed in this land.

"Oh, Danny! That revelation sparked hope within my breast that one day... one day I *would* be free. From that time on, I waited for the right time to make my escape. It would not be easy. In slave states, a Negro by himself had to have a pass from his master stating his business if he left his owner's property, or he would be thrown in jail. I had to be able to write exceedingly well so that I could write my own pass... and so I practiced on whatever piece of bark or wood I had, using charcoal from the fire—

and then burned the wood to cover up my skill.

"Master Hugh and Mistress Sophia were quite religious and made sure their whole household attended the Methodist church regularly. The preacher taught the straight Bible, and in this way I learned that all men were sinners—black and white alike—and that God had sent His Son, Jesus, to pay the price for our sins. I had not yet tasted the lash—that was yet to come—but back at the old plantation when I was just a child, I had seen the backs of grown men ripped open in blood for their 'sins.' So to hear that Jesus took a whipping and then was nailed to an ugly cross *for my sins* moved me deep in my soul. I couldn't imagine anyone doing that for a slave.

"About the age of thirteen, I sincerely wanted to know that I was right with God. Fortunately for me, an old, godly deacon took this fatherless boy under his wing and showed me how to find God. He was a freedman but could barely read himself, so I read his Bible to him, and in this way he taught me. Master Hugh found out about my meetings with old George Lawson and forbade it—but he never did anything about it, and so I continued to be taught by the old man.

"The thing about learning... it's not something you can keep to yourself. No sooner did I learn how to read, or how to write the alphabet, than I was teaching other black children in our Baltimore neighborhood. Secretly, of course, or my experience with the whip would have started at an earlier age.

"I had a cousin older than I—Henny was her name—and she had fallen into a fire as a child. Her hands were badly burned, and when the scars healed, the skin pulled tight, turning her hands into nearly useless claws. My legal master, Captain Thomas, also sent Henny to his brother Hugh, hoping to be rid of her. But not finding a useful niche for Henny in his Baltimore household, Hugh Auld sent her back to his brother. In a fit of temper, Thomas Auld said, 'If you don't want Henny, you can't have Fred, either,' and demanded that Master Hugh send me back to St. Michael's.

"What a change in my circumstances! In Baltimore, my life was not my own, but I had never gone hungry. Master Thomas, however, was a stingy man and fed his 'property' just enough to keep us alive. I took to stealing food from the Aulds' full storerooms to ease the constant pinch in my stomach. At first, I really struggled with my conscience, because I knew stealing was wrong. But my conscience also argued that it was Master Thomas who was withholding food he should rightfully give his slaves, and also that with a full stomach I could do better work for my master.

"I do not condone stealing, Danny. But it was a lot to ask of a young boy being systematically starved by a highly respected citizen.

"So I was quite interested when Master Thomas fell under conviction at a Methodist camp meeting when I was about fifteen. People came from far and near, setting up tents in a large circle in an open pasture. Beyond the tents—which had all the comforts of home, including slaves and servants—were the wagons and oxcarts of ordinary people and bonfires to cook huge pots of food to feed the assembly. Directly in front of the preacher's platform was a 'pen' where mourners could kneel, and one night from my position behind the platform, where the black folks sat, I saw an amazing sight: Master Thomas making his way through the crowd and falling to his knees in the mourner's pen. This interested me and my fellow slaves greatly. Could this religious conversion mean a positive change in our treatment by the Aulds? Dared we hope Thomas Auld might even emancipate his slaves, as sometimes happened by a man under deep spiritual conviction?

"But we were bitterly disappointed. Oh, Captain Thomas had got religion, all right. He became a pillar of the church and was soon a Class Leader. Household prayers morning and night became standard routine. But the tears of conviction, the shouts of praise, the dance of joy that we witnessed at the camp meeting made not a whit of difference in the miserly amount of food doled out to us or in any other detail of our slavery. Nor would he allow me or any other slave to attend church or be instructed in the Bible. Indeed, this was the general attitude of all white people I knew... with one exception.

"Not long after the camp meeting, a pious young man named Wilson asked if I would help instruct a little Sunday school at the house of a free colored man. Of course, this had to be done secretly, but I eagerly responded, feeling that now I would be doing something useful with my life. But at our second meeting, while teaching several colored children to read the Gospel, Thomas Auld and two other men stormed into the house armed with sticks. They drove us out and told us never to meet again. As for me, I was accused of wanting to be another Nat Turner, and if I persisted in my rebellion, I would meet the same end.

"By this time, my own religious convictions had been badly shaken. Didn't the Bible say God could change the hearts of men? Yet Thomas Auld seemed as mean, if not meaner, *after* his conversion as before. Of this I was sure when he decided to farm out my services for a year to a certain Mr. Covey—a man with a well-earned reputation as a 'slave-breaker.' Mr. Covey, to his credit, did not starve the slaves rented out to him. For a change, I had plenty to eat. But I had plenty of other troubles. For it seemed no matter how hard I tried to do what I was told, something was always wrong with it, and I felt the whip for the first time. Not a week went by that I wasn't beaten. Mr. Covey was always watching—even when we couldn't see him. He would creep up behind us in the field, or sneak behind the stable, to suddenly appear and yell about our laziness or blame us for poor pickings in the field. I was told to do tasks for which I had no experience—such as driving a yoke of unbroken oxen into the woods to get firewood—and then beaten when the stubborn creatures ran away, dumped the wood, and broke the cart.

"After a particularly vicious beating during harvest, after I became sick and fainted in the intense summer heat, I decided to run away—back to Master Thomas. I decided to appeal to the slave-owner's own reasoning, that his 'property' was being abused and would soon be ruined. But Master Thomas presumed I was feigning sickness to get out of working and ordered me back to Mr. Covey straightaway or risk being sold 'down South.'

"As I made my way through the woods back to the Covey farm, I had time to think. I did not believe myself to be lazy or incompetent—all the things of which I was often accused. I determined to fulfill every task given to me willingly and to the best of my ability... and if I was *still* beaten, I would stand up against the man. What did I have to lose? The worst Covey could do was kill me—but if I was to be killed, I determined to die with a shred of dignity.

"I came back on a Sunday. Covey, too, was a church-going man, and he allowed his slaves a day of rest. But early Monday morning, even before daylight, Covey dragged me out of bed to feed and curry the horses. I reminded myself of my determination to fulfill every request, no matter how unreasonable, so I set out for the stable in quick time. As I was going up the ladder into the loft to get hay for the horses, Covey snuck up behind me and pulled me down by the legs. He had a rope in his hands and I knew he intended to tie me up and beat me—for what reason, I had no idea. But to his shock, I resisted him—and for the next two hours

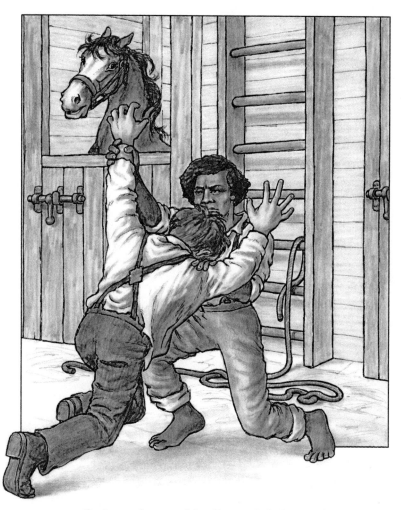

we wrestled on the stable floor. I did not fight back
to injure him—only to defend myself and keep from
being beaten.

"At length, exhausted, Covey shook me off and
growled, 'Now, you scoundrel, go to your work; I
would not have whipped you half so hard if you had

not resisted.' But he knew—and he knew that *I* knew—that he had not whipped me at all. And never again in the remaining time I was with Mr. Covey did he lay a finger on me, though he blustered and threatened.

"To my surprise, Mr. Covey did not tell Captain Thomas about my resistance—nor did he let it be known to anyone else. Resisting one's master could have gotten me hung. But he was humiliated that he had been bested by a mere sixteen-year-old boy and did not want that fact to ruin his reputation.

"Danny, I can hardly describe what I felt as I watched Covey stomp off to the house. It was the turning point in my life as a slave. I was *nothing* before; I was a *man* now. It renewed my self-respect and self-confidence. I had reached a point where I was not afraid to die—would rather die, in fact, than not stand up for my dignity and worth as a human being. And that gave me the spirit of a *free man*, even though I was still a slave."

Frederick Douglass's story was interrupted as the New York Central pulled into Albany. Danny had been so caught up in the story that he'd hardly noticed when the conductor came through the car, lighting the gas lamps as twilight blanketed the countryside. Now people were starting to stand up, gathering their bags and bundles as the train jerked and squealed to a stop. Some of the passengers were going on to New York; the rest were changing to the Boston & Albany line.

Settled once more in a passenger car on the train heading for Boston, Mr. Douglass dozed with his chin on his chest as Danny peered into the darkness, thinking about the story he'd been told. It stirred something deep inside him, like part of him waking up after a long sleep. But he felt confused, too. He'd always thought of the Douglasses as a God-fearing family. But he'd heard something in Mr. Douglass's tone—a bitter irony—as he related the cruelty of Captain Thomas and Mr. Covey... who both claimed to be Christians. Seeing his companion yawn and shift in his seat, Danny blurted, "After what your masters did to you, didn't you hate Christianity?"

Frederick Douglass's eyes shot open. He seemed instantly awake. "That's a good question, Danny, and deserves an honest answer. I love the Christianity *of Christ* who inspired His followers to visit the orphan, the widow, and the prisoner, who forgives the sinner, who gave His very life for all mankind. I only despise the hypocritical Christianity of the slave-owner, who teaches Sunday school class on Sunday but whips women and old men, stripped half-naked in the sun, on Monday; who gathers the household for morning and evening prayers but steals the wages of his laborers, sells children away from their parents, and refuses to let those entrusted to him read the Holy Bible for themselves."

A few passengers looked their way, frowning. It was hard to miss Frederick Douglass's resonant voice. But as the train rocked and clacked its way toward Boston, the man dozed once more, leaving Danny alone with his thoughts. I was nothing before; I was a man now, Douglass had said. *I had reached a point where I was not afraid to die—would rather die, in fact, than not stand up for my dignity and worth as a human being.*

What did it mean? Why had Mr. Douglass told him this story? He wanted to ask, but Mr. Douglass slept until the train pulled into the Boston station. Danny's spirits sank. He should feel glad to see his uncle—but he didn't want to be banished from the Douglass home. What a fool he'd been to be such a slacker the past few months!

But now it was too late.

Chapter 6

Raise the Flag, Boys!

WHERE WAS UNCLE THOMAS? Danny tried to peer through a sea of parasols, hoop skirts, and top hats. What was going on here? White folks, black folks—all dressed in their Sunday best. But in the entire crowd he couldn't see his uncle.

"Keep up, Danny!" Mr. Douglass ordered. "We can't miss this next train."

Next train? What was Mr. Douglass talking about? Hadn't they come to Boston to meet his uncle? But there was no time for questions. Douglass had been swallowed up in the crowd that seemed to be moving like a giant slug toward a door on the far side of the station. Danny shoved and squeezed, hanging on to his bag for dear life as he tried to catch up. He glanced at the sign over the door leading out onto the far platform—Boston & Providence Railroad—just as he was sucked through the narrow opening and spit out on the other side.

"Danny! Over here!"

Danny made his way toward Mr. Douglass's voice, and together they pushed their way onto one of the train cars. Hundreds of other people crammed into the cars, far more than the number of seats. But the mood seemed good-natured, even jovial. And to Danny's surprise, many people greeted Mr. Douglass by name.

"Frederick! Good to see you." A glance at Danny. "One of your boys?"

"Mr. Douglass! That was a great speech about the Emancipation Proclamation on New Year's Day!"

"Congratulations, Mr. Douglass. I hear two of your sons joined the Fifty-Fourth Massachusetts. You must be proud today!"

Today? Danny was bewildered. What was today?

The Boston & Providence jerked and chugged out of Boston's South Station. Women grabbed their bonnets, and Danny grabbed the back of a seat. Frederick Douglass, grinning broadly beneath his mustache, seemed to be enjoying himself—and Danny's bewilderment—greatly.

The chatter in the train car competed with the loud whistles of the train. Danny strained to pick up words and phrases from the conversations around him: *Readville... Camp Meigs... presentation... flags... historic event...*

So that's where this train was headed! To Camp Meigs, where the Fifty-Fourth Massachusetts Infantry had been training for months. But... all these people were going to Camp Meigs? They acted like they were going to a festival. The excitement was contagious, and Danny felt giddy with anticipation. Would they get to see Lewis and Charles? What was happening today?

Compared to their train trip across New York, the ride to Readville was relatively short. Hundreds of people poured from the train, like beans spilling from a torn sack. Soldiers in "Union blue" scurried in and out of the crowd. He wanted to gawk, but Frederick Douglass was heading for a wooden platform draped in red, white, and blue banners, and Danny had to hustle with his hop-step, hop-step to keep up. At the bottom of the wooden steps leading up to the platform, Danny hesitated. The stand looked full of men in top hats and women in expensive dresses. But Mr. Douglass mouthed, "Stick by me, Danny," and headed up the steps. Hauling his bag, Danny followed.

As he stepped onto the platform behind the railings, Danny's mouth dropped open. He couldn't help it. Never had he seen a sight like the spectacle before him.

A long field stretched out like a green carpet. Hundreds—maybe thousands—of visitors stood along each side. Yellow, blue, green, and pink parasols dotted the crowd like colored sugar sprinkles. The Fifty-Fourth Massachusetts Infantry, one thousand strong, stood by companies of one hundred in the bright May sunshine, noncommissioned officers at their head. Shades of brown, black, and tan colored every proud face of the foot soldiers.

"Danny," Douglass's voice interrupted, "I want you to meet Governor Andrew."

Danny turned reluctantly, as though the regiment might disappear if he didn't fasten it with his eyes. A dignified white man, somewhat portly, extended his hand. "Pleased to meet you, Danny Sims. I have met your uncle Thomas. An up-and-coming young man!"

Danny shook the man's hand, but words stuck in his throat. Douglass was already turning to a couple of other gentlemen on the stand. "Wendell Phillips... William Lloyd Garrison..." Douglass nodded gravely to each in turn.

Danny's eyes widened. The two famous abolitionists who had taken the young Frederick Douglass under their wing and given him a platform for his passionate speeches nodded politely. Now Douglass had made a name for himself on his own and dared to disagree with Garrison over his stance that the U.S. Constitution was "pro-slavery."

A slight smile tugged at one corner of Danny's mouth, remembering the namesakes of these two—"Wendell" and "William"—enjoying the pasture back in Rochester.

Turning back to the field, Danny scanned the companies closest to the viewing stand, hoping to catch a glimpse of Lewis or Charles. Each soldier stood at parade rest, resting the butts of their gleaming rifles on the ground. Behind him he caught snatches of conversation: "Some folks are going to be mighty uncomfortable seeing a whole regiment of armed blacks."... "At least they didn't have to break into an armory to get *those* rifles!"—a reference, Danny guessed, to John Brown's ill-fated raid on the armory at Harper's Ferry... "Humph. Those Enfields take forty-five seconds to reload—they'll get more use from their bayonets once they get into battle...."

Something stirred the crowd. From the right, mounted officers—all white—rode in formation in front of the Fifty-Fourth. An order rang out, and immediately the entire regiment snapped to attention, their heels together and rifles on their right shoulders. The officers turned their horses and stopped in front of the viewing stand. A loud murmur rose from the crowd, then hushed, but not before Danny heard from behind him: "There's Colonel Shaw."... "Only two weeks married, I hear."... "Done a fine job if what we see before us is any proof."... "I see he's tapped his friend Ned Hallowell as his second-in-command."

Danny stared at the officer whose horse stood front and center of the line of officers. So this was Colonel Robert Gould Shaw, commander of the Fifty-Fourth! But he barely looked twenty-five—not even as old as Uncle Thomas! A sandy-colored mustache dusted the young man's upper lip, and a tuft of hair decorated his chin. But Danny noted the expert way

the colonel sat his dark chestnut horse... what a fine
piece of horseflesh! The chestnut was finely muscled,
strong without extra weight, its mane and tail carefully brushed. The horse was alert but not skittish.
Danny felt an immediate bond. Here was a man who
loved a fine horse.

Governor Andrew stepped forward, and the oc-
casion for the day's festivities became apparent:
presentation of the regimental flags. Danny watched

in awe as the first flag was brought forth—the red, white, and blue United States flag with its thirty-four stars. As a handsome young man stepped from the ranks to receive the flagstaff, Danny saw moisture glisten on Frederick Douglass's cheek. *There is no power on earth which can deny that he has earned the right to citizenship in the United States!*—that's what Douglass had said about blacks serving in the Union army.

The second flag was the white flag of Massachusetts, with its blue shield and the figure of a Massachuset Indian holding a bow and arrow pointed downward in a symbol of peace. Governor Andrew thundered the words emblazoned on the flag: "By the Sword We Seek Peace, but Peace Only Under Liberty!" Another young man with two corporal's stripes stepped forward to receive the flag.

Then came two more flags—the Goddess of Liberty on white silk with the motto, "Liberty, Loyalty, and Unity," and a blue flag with a white Christian cross—before Governor Andrew made his speech. It was obvious that Andrew's political reputation rested on the success of this regiment—and just as obvious that he had confidence in the newly formed "colored regiment." "I know not," he thundered, "when, in all human history, to any given thousand men in arms there has been committed a work at once so proud, so precious, so full of hope and glory as the work committed to you." Sweeping an arm to indicate the entire regiment, the governor added: "I have confidence which knows no hesitation or doubt that you will do your duty."

A crisp breeze caught the flags and they snapped out full, flowing like liquid waves as Colonel Shaw responded with a short speech. "These men understand the importance of the undertaking," he told those on the viewing stand. "We only hope for an opportunity to show that you have not made a mistake in entrusting the honor of the State to a colored regiment."

After the speeches, the entire regiment entertained the visitors with drills on the parade ground and then was dismissed to greet their families and friends. "Father!" yelled familiar voices—and there were Charles and Lewis. Danny stared. Lewis had the stripes of a sergeant major on his sleeve. For once in his life, Mr. Douglass seemed speechless. Lewis grinned. "Yes, sir! The highest rank of any colored enlisted man. Not bad for a *start*." He winked at Danny. "Come on, we'll give you a tour of the camp."

The foursome walked through the camp as Douglass's sons pointed out the cookhouse, the blacksmithy, the quartermaster's supply house, officer's quarters, and the ten wooden barracks holding a hundred soldiers each. Danny was surprised to see a number of boys, a few even younger than himself, wearing Union blue.

"Who are they?" he hissed at Charles, jerking his head toward a boy jogging through the camp carrying a packet and another leading two horses to a water trough.

"Runners, orderlies, drummer boys—you name it," Charles said casually.

"Boys who are standing up for themselves," Douglass murmured in his ear.

A brief hope surged upward in Danny's spirit—then crumbled like dust. Was this a cruel joke? Why would the Douglasses throw this in his face—knowing he was lame and could never join the army?

"I have an appointment with Colonel Shaw," Douglass said shortly. "Where are the colonel's quarters, Charles?" Danny followed, hands stuffed in his pockets, aware once more of his awkward gait. His own private gloom shadowed the day.

Colonel Shaw was greeting visitors underneath a canopy just outside his quarters. On seeing Frederick Douglass, however, he excused himself and held out his hand. "Mr. Douglass! I am indeed honored."

Danny hung back but Mr. Douglass pulled him forward. "This is the boy I wrote to you about, Colonel," Mr. Douglass said. "Danny Sims. He's top-notch with horses—and I hear you don't want just anyone looking after your prize."

Danny felt heat rise in his face as Colonel Shaw looked him over. "Indeed! Good with horses, are you?"

"Y-yes, sir," Danny stammered. Was the colonel suggesting—?

Colonel Shaw clasped his gloved hands behind his back. "I was quite dismayed when my orderly got sick and had to be sent home. Then Sergeant Major Douglass"—he nodded at Lewis—"told me he knew

69

a young man who could do the job. So I wrote to Mr. Douglass, here, who seems to agree. But I give you fair warning, young man—I permit no tomfoolery in my command. I need someone who can not only take care of my steed but my person, as well." He uttered a short laugh, indicating the double row of brass buttons up and down his uniform jacket. "What do you think, Danny? Up for the job?"

Dumbfounded, Danny looked at Mr. Douglass, who nodded, then at Lewis and Charles, who were grinning from ear to ear. Taking a deep breath, he stood a little taller and puffed out his chest. "I can do it, sir."

Just then one of the infantrymen—older than most of the others, Danny noted—strode under the canopy and saluted the colonel.

Colonel Shaw frowned. "What is it, Sergeant Vogelsang?"

The man handed him a sheet of paper. "Orders, sir. Just came in on the wire from Secretary of War Stanton."

Wide-eyed, Danny held his breath as the colonel read the paper and then looked up. A look of triumph lit up the man's face. "The Fifty-Fourth Massachusetts is ordered to report to General Hunter at Hilton Head, South Carolina—at once."

Chapter 7

Running the Gauntlet

DANNY HAD HAD FAIR WARNING, but it didn't take long to learn it for fact: Colonel Shaw was a hard taskmaster. As the colonel's new orderly and groom, Danny was up before dawn to feed, water, and curry Shaw's horses—Shaw had several for his personal use—then he had to brush the colonel's uniform, lay it out, polish his boots, and make sure the commander had a clean shirt for the day. Everything had to be done *before* the colonel needed it; Shaw had no time to waste on waiting. The Fifty-Fourth was on the move.

Danny had barely finished helping Shaw get dressed on the first day when a young private showed up at the colonel's quarters and saluted.

"You sent for me, sir?"

"At ease, Private Caldwell. You can read?"

"Yes, sir. And write, too, sir."

"Hmm. Good. I want you to give my orderly a crash course in army regulations, military protocol, names and ranks of all the officers—everything you've had two months to learn, he needs to learn in two days. And get him in a uniform."

The young private grinned. "Yes, *sir*! Now, sir?"

"Yes, now. Danny, be back at eleven o'clock sharp to saddle Regent."

Shaw had said nothing about Danny's lame foot; he simply gave him his duties and expected them to be carried out. But Private Caldwell was more blunt. "What happened to your foot?" he demanded as Danny resorted to his quick hop-step, hop-step to keep up with his new tutor.

"Born with it." Danny was relieved to speak the words. He *knew* people noticed his clubfoot; might as well be honest about it.

Private Caldwell shrugged. "Name's James Caldwell. Call me Jim—but don't tell my grandmother." He laughed. "She's the one who got to name me and called me James, like the apostle. Wants me to be a preacher. But our family doesn't need another preacher—that woman is preacher enough!"

That piqued Danny's curiosity. "Your grandmother is a preacher?"

"Oh, she preaches, all right. You may have heard of her: Sojourner Truth."

Danny's eyes widened. Who hadn't heard of

Sojourner Truth? The woman was a legend in abolitionist circles, giving her "testimony" about Jesus and speaking powerfully about the evils of slavery even though she had never had a day of formal education.

James's first stop was the quartermaster, where Danny was outfitted with a navy jacket, cap, and sky blue wool trousers. No boots would fit his deformed foot—his own battered shoes would have to do. Danny's skin prickled as he stripped off his worn and patched clothes and put on the Union uniform—like shedding his old skin and emerging somehow new and magnificent. But James gave him no time for self-admiration. Grabbing a regulation manual, the young private drilled Danny for two hours on how to salute, how to address an officer, where to stand. The details seemed endless.

By eleven o'clock, Danny had Regent saddled and ready for Colonel Shaw, who left him with cleanup detail of his quarters and exercising the relief horses. *Tomfoolery?* Danny snorted to himself as he scrubbed the worn wooden floor of Shaw's office and sleeping room. *Who had time for tomfoolery?*

For the next several days, the entire regiment was pushed to double activity. Supply wagons arriving daily with tents, haversacks, canteens, and ammunition had to be unloaded, checked against a master list, and repacked for travel. Each company drilled daily, including long marches in the countryside under heavy knapsacks. Men who performed well were moved up a notch in rank. Those who were caught slacking, complaining, or disobeying a rule spent a day doing hard labor or in chains in the camp brig.

Danny rarely saw Charles but caught regular glimpses of Sergeant Major Lewis Douglass, who was part of Shaw's staff that oversaw the entire regiment. By day's end, he was exhausted, and his lame foot ached with the added activity. He was grateful for the darkness as the men gathered around campfires at night so he could loosen his shoe and rub his sore muscles. A few harmonicas came out of jacket pockets, and the air filled with music—rousing camp songs, old spirituals, reverent hymns. The nearest campfire might pick up the same song, calling back the refrain. The camp had two black chaplains—Reverend Jackson and Reverend Grimes—who went from campfire to campfire, barrack to barrack, each evening to pray with the men.

As firelight flickered from face to face, the soldiers, so highly disciplined during the day, let down their guard. "Glad they're not shipping us out from New York," a sergeant named Simmons muttered one night. "Our first battle might be on free soil."

"Wha' you talkin' 'bout, man?"

"My sister lives there. Wrote me that the Irish are kicking up a fuss about being conscripted into the army. Saying this isn't *their* war. Blaming black folks. Things are pretty tense."

"No kidding." A look passed from face to face. "But Boston's okay, right? I mean, look at all the folks who've been visiting us at Camp Meigs. Everybody seems to like what they see."

Simmons shrugged. "But we're leaving Camp Meigs. Gonna be marching through downtown Boston. Who knows how the general population gonna react when they see the north's first regiment of free blacks armed just like the white regiments."

Silence held the private thoughts of the men as they stared into the campfire. Then the mournful notes of a harmonica lifted on the soft May evening.

"Easy, boy... easy," soothed Danny as he coaxed Regent up the wooden ramp into the train car at the Readville station. Ten days after the presentation of the flags, the Fifty-Fourth Massachusetts was loading up and heading for Boston, where they would transfer to a troop ship in Boston harbor. One by one, the officers' horses had been loaded into the stable car by their respective grooms. Regent was the last to go up.

The horses had caught the general excitement and tension, and the grooms had their hands full keeping them calm as the train jerked and steamed its way out of the station. Danny made sure each of his charges was tied securely, laying a calming hand on twitching necks and murmuring softly. When he came back to Regent, the horse nickered and nuzzled Danny's chest with his soft velvet nose. In the ten days since Danny had been appointed as groom for Shaw's horses, he had spent every minute he could spare getting to know the colonel's prize. Regent had been wary at first but warmed to Danny's constant attention. Now Danny's presence seemed to calm the horse, even though the floor under his feet rattled and quaked over the rails.

Danny leaned his head against the chestnut's warm neck as the regiment pulled away from the safety of Camp Meigs and headed into the unknown. Word of the growing tension in northern cities over involuntary conscription sobered the men of the Fifty-Fourth. Danny had seen it in their eyes as the sons of Frederick Douglass and the grandson of Sojourner Truth gave him a curt nod on the way to the troop cars that morning. These were the sons and grandsons of former slaves who had spoken out boldly for the cause of freedom for the millions still in slavery. Danny knew all the men of the Fifty-Fourth were willing to put their lives on the line. But they were worried, too. Would the white regiments allow them to fight side by side in their common cause? Would Union generals give them the opportunity to prove themselves on the battlefield?

And the first unspoken test: Would the people of Boston jeer or cheer as they marched through the streets today?

As the train steamed into Boston's station and the doors of the stable car slid open, one of the other stable boys muttered: "Well, boys, today we run the gauntlet."

A line of wagons was waiting to unload the regiment's supplies and take them to the dock. Danny brought a nervous Regent to Colonel Shaw, who put his foot into the stirrup and swung into the saddle. "Mount up!" he ordered his officers. "Parade formation!" Men and women along the street stopped and stared as the regiment's ten companies quickly formed.

With the regimental flags flying at the front of the column to the cadence of the drums, followed by Colonel Shaw and his staff officers, the Fifty-Fourth Massachusetts began the march from the train station to Boston Common, where they would be reviewed by Governor Andrew. Each enlisted man had shined his boots and his rifle to spit-and-polish, and they were a sight to behold: shoulders back, heads high, eyes straight ahead, unloaded rifles on their shoulders. And—if Danny's own rapidly beating heart was any clue—tense with uncertainty about their reception.

Danny and the other orderlies and grooms brought up the rear, leading the relief horses, followed by the supply wagons. *Ta-rum-tum-tum! Ta-rum-tum-tum.* Far ahead they could hear the drums and the *tramp, tramp* of a thousand pairs of boots. Oh, how Danny wished he could ride! Not only to relieve the embarrassment of his awkward hop-step, hop-step in front of gaping strangers, but so he could see what was happening ahead!

As the long column made its way—*ta-rum-tum-tum!*—toward Boston Common, marching five abreast in the middle of the street past banks and businesses, shops and hotels, Danny heard a noise ahead, rolling toward them, getting louder and

louder. He anxiously sneaked a glance at his fellow grooms, who gripped their lead ropes tighter. Glancing up, he saw men and women leaning out of windows, shouting words he could not understand. Then he saw arms waving handkerchiefs back and forth from windows, and hats waving in the air above the growing crowd collecting on the sidewalks. With a surge of astonishment, Danny realized what he heard rising above the drums and marching feet:

The people of Boston were cheering!

"Hooray for the Fifty-Fourth!"

"Make 'em run, boys!"

"God bless Massachusetts!"

And somewhere in the crowd a voice roared, "Look at 'em! Marching forth to blot out the sins of the nation!"

Danny forgot his throbbing foot. He seemed to float between the two horses he was leading as the regiment began to fill Boston Common. But suddenly, above the drums, above the boots on cobblestones, above the cheers, he heard his name.

"Danny! Danny Sims!"

Jerking his head to the left, then to the right, Danny scanned the crowd on either side of the street. Again he heard his name: "Danny! Danny Sims! Over here!" There! He caught sight of his uncle Thomas, hat waving in the air.

And tears streaming down his face.

Chapter 8

Deep South

DANNY HARDLY REMEMBERED ANYTHING ELSE about the ceremony in Boston Commons or the remainder of the march to the harbor. Uncle Thomas's tears seemed to wash away every minor distraction and focused his mind. Twelve years ago, his uncle had been hunted down, dragged out of one of these buildings, *marched in chains through these very streets,* taken to the harbor, and shipped down South.

Back to brutal slavery.

But today, May 28, 1863, Thomas had stood on these same streets a free man—like Frederick Douglass, he had bought his own freedom—watching a regiment of black soldiers, trained and armed, marching in the cause of freedom. Lewis and Charles Douglass, Peter Vogelsang, Robert Simmons, James Caldwell—and hundreds like them—had *volunteered* to head into the bosom of slavery for one purpose only: to free millions of slaves who still could not call one moment, one breath, even one child their own.

And Danny was going with them.

The *DeMolay*, a steam-powered troop ship, lay waiting for them at Battery Wharf. Loading began shortly after noon—each man eating what he could from his haversack of hardtack, cheese, dried meat, and water from his canteen—and was finished by four o'clock. The horses were among the first to board. Regent and the other horses were blindfolded and coaxed up the special gangplank into the hold. Danny was amazed that Colonel Shaw entrusted him with this delicate duty, but he vowed under his breath to let nothing happen to this beautiful animal. Once aboard, the horses were stabled belowdecks in beds of deep straw, given hay and water, and their grooms were given strict instructions not to leave their sides until the ship was underway.

So Danny could feel—but not see—the *DeMolay* pull away from the dock, turn about, steam out of Boston's harbor, and head for the open sea.

For six days, the *DeMolay* plowed through choppy waters, always with the Atlantic seacoast within sight along the starboard horizon. It was impossible to tell one state from another as they slipped past Massachusetts, Rhode Island, Connecticut, New York, New Jersey, Delaware, Maryland, Virginia, North Carolina...

But on the morning of June 3, every man and boy of the Fifty-Fourth Massachusetts lined the railing of the ship, watching silently as the *DeMolay* steamed past the federal blockade of Charleston Bay. Danny edged his way through the men, standing four and five deep, until he pressed against the rail. Beyond the Union gun ships, he could see Fort Sumter, now in Confederate hands.

"Recapture that fort," muttered a familiar voice in Danny's ear, "and we unlock the gate to the heart of the Confederacy."

Danny looked over his shoulder and up into the face of Lewis Douglass. The sergeant major stood behind him, his eyes hard as the fort slid past in the distance.

"Charleston," breathed Danny. Somewhere beyond the fort lay the legendary southern city of grand mansions, elegant cypress trees, genteel southern ladies and gentlemen—and the largest slave market in North America.

"That's where this war started, and that's where it's going to end." Lewis spit out the words. "I, for one, plan to march through its streets and tear that auction block apart with my bare hands."

On the dock at St. Simons Island, Danny bent over a water barrel he was using as a makeshift desk as he studied the letter he was writing to Rose Parker back in Rochester. Georgia in June was already sultry, and small rivers of sweat ran down his back, but he didn't dare strip off his shirt; Colonel Shaw might need him at any time. Dipping his pen, he continued writing carefully so as not to waste paper.

...Everyone's wondering when we get to fight! Haven't seen anything of the enemy. I know you'll say not to ask for trouble—but so far all they think we're good for is fatigue duty. Unloading ships, digging latrines, clearing land—you name it, we've done it. But when the Fifty-Fourth was ordered to clean the camp of a white regiment, Shaw got mad! Oh, Rose, it was beautiful to see. He'd trained these men to fight, not be servants to white troops. So when he heard that Colonel Montgomery was heading for Georgia with the Second South Carolina Volunteers—mostly ex-slaves he recruited on raids into Confederate territory—Shaw asked if the Fifty-Fourth could join him on any campaigns.

So here we are. St. Simons Island, Georgia—got here yesterday, June 9. If the Rebels don't get us, these pesky flies might do it. Flies in the dog tent, flies in my shirt, flies all over my food. Say, Rose, I sure do miss your cooking. What I wouldn't give for—

"Colonel Shaw!"

Danny jerked his head up. Who was yelling for the colonel? A small steamer had pulled up to the dock. On the deck, a small, lean man in his late forties with a long beard and a colonel's insignia on his sleeve called out, "Get Colonel Shaw, boy!"

Danny ran and in two minutes was back with

Shaw. "Colonel Montgomery!" said the younger officer. "What can I—"

"How soon can you be ready to start on an expedition?" Montgomery demanded.

Colonel Shaw repressed a grin. "In half an hour!"

Eight companies of the Fifty-Fourth had loaded onto a small troop transport and headed north along the coast to Altamaha Sound, while two companies stayed behind to guard the camp. At the mouth of the Altamaha, they met up with another troop ship carrying five companies from Montgomery's regiment and one section from the Third Rhode Island Artillery. By morning, two gunships had joined them.

Shaw had debated leaving Danny behind to take care of Regent and his relief horses, then decided his orderly would be useful to him if he went along. Danny was glad not to be left behind as the flotilla headed upriver. Like the enlisted men, all his senses were alert as the ships slid past huge oaks hung with Spanish moss, through which they could glimpse houses along the picturesque waterway.

"Fire at will!" roared Montgomery's voice from the troop ship ahead of them.

"What?" Shaw seemed stunned at the order. Nobody had fired at them. In fact, Danny, standing closeby, hadn't seen any Confederate soldiers at all.

But the gunboats started shelling the homes as

they passed. Danny could tell the men of the Fifty-Fourth were uneasy. He knew what they must be thinking: What if there were women and children in there? "Fire!" roared Montgomery. The Enfield rifles came up and fired—into clumps of trees, it looked like to Danny—and the men took longer than usual to tamp and reload. Not so much as a pea-shooter fired back.

"I'd heard the man was a loose cannon," Shaw muttered, sucking in his breath, "but I didn't want to believe it."

Ten miles upriver, the two troop ships eased up to the docks alongside the town of Darien. The place looked totally deserted—of civilians, as well as any Confederate units that might have been lodged there. "Just as well," Colonel Shaw muttered to Lieutenant Colonel Hallowell as the men prepared to disembark. "They certainly had plenty of notice that we were coming." His mouth twisted in disgust.

Darien was located on a bluff overlooking the river. As the troops scrambled up the steep paths and regrouped in the public square of the town, Danny stayed one step behind Shaw in case he was needed. As Shaw and Montgomery talked quietly, he looked up and down the main street, amazed at the beauty of the town. Beyond the storehouses and several mills along the riverbank, he could see elegant houses lining the side streets, the steeples of several churches, a courthouse, a school, and stores for dry goods, produce, harnesses, and hardware. Overarching the streets were magnificent oaks and mulberry trees.

Colonel Shaw's rising voice registered in Danny's brain. "Take *all* things of value?" Shaw was saying. "I thought General Hunter's orders were to seize food and property that might be useful to our army and destroy anything that might aid the rebellion. But homes, churches, household goods, personal items— these were to remain untouched."

Montgomery shrugged. "That's your interpretation, Colonel." He turned to his troops of the Second South Carolina. "Disperse! Ransack the buildings! Take anything of value you can load on the ships." In an instant, Montgomery's recently freed slaves-turned-soldiers began to run gleefully through the streets, breaking into buildings and dragging out chairs, mirrors, oil paintings, tools, bedding... even a piano.

Shaw turned on his heel and gave terse orders to the Fifty-Fourth. "Lieutenant Colonel Hallowell, Sergeant Lieutenant Colonel Douglass—divide the companies into ranks, each with a commanding officer. Search the warehouses, barns, and stores. Bring out foodstuffs, livestock, and any goods useful to us in camp. Take nothing for yourselves."

As the two regiments fanned out in their quest to plunder the town—one helter-skelter, like street toughs looting a city after a riot, the other disciplined, methodical, and restrained—the holds of the ships at the docks below began to fill with cotton, lumber, grain, salt pork, and other foodstuffs, as well as a ridiculous pile of curtains, chairs, rugs, and china.

Danny hovered near Colonel
Shaw, who paced in the open square under the relent-
less sun. He tried to bring the colonel a dipperful of
water from a nearby water barrel, but Shaw waved
it away.

Finally the troops reassembled in the square.
Colonel Shaw tapped his foot, waiting for the order
to return to the ships. Standing nearby, Danny saw
Montgomery lean toward Shaw and say in a quiet,

determined voice, "I shall burn this town."

Colonel Shaw reacted as if he had been slapped. "Unthinkable, Colonel Montgomery! We have not one reason to cause such wanton destruction."

Montgomery's eyes narrowed. "These Southerners must be made to feel that this is a real war!" he snapped. "They started this rebellion. Now they will be swept away by the hand of God like the Jews of old."

Shaw drew himself up and faced his adversary. "Hand of God? Thuggery is more like it! I will have no part in it."

Montgomery shrugged. "Suit yourself." He strode out, barking orders at his troops, who once again fanned out, this time with hastily made torches. The Fifty-Fourth milled around the square anxiously as smoke and flames began to fill the courthouse, the stately homes—some built in the colonial era—and even churches along Darien's empty streets. Not satisfied that the job was being done fast enough, Montgomery ordered out one company of the Fifty-Fourth, who followed reluctantly, perfectly aware of their own colonel's feelings on the matter.

Montgomery's men poured turpentine on the cotton and other goods in the storehouses that they hadn't been able to load onto the ships and set them afire. A breeze sprang up, fanning the flames into a roaring furnace. Black smoke billowed into the air. The Union troops backed down the steep paths to the river and scrambled onto their ships.

Casting off, the steam engines sprang to life,

pushing the ships out into the river and away from the intense heat. The flotilla headed back downriver toward the sea, leaving the fiery destruction behind them.

Shaw was seething with anger. Danny could hear him in his cabin, ranting to his friend Ned Hallowell that the raid was "a dirty piece of business... burning and pillaging is piracy, not war!" When Lieutenant Colonel Hallowell finally came out, Danny slipped in and found Shaw sitting on his bunk, head in his hands. Not knowing what else to do, he knelt and began to pull off the colonel's boots.

"Ohhh, Danny," the colonel groaned. "When word leaks out about this dirty raid, heads will wag both North and South. They'll call us barbarians!—feeding right into the hands of those who don't think a black regiment belongs in the Union army."

Danny didn't reply. When the colonel finally fell into a restless slumber, Danny curled up on his bed-roll on the floor of the cabin. There were no songs on the deck that night. Perhaps every man in the Fifty-Fourth felt as he did... ashamed of what had happened that day. Was *this* war? Was any slave closer to freedom this day because of what had happened here?

Chapter 9

Battle on James Island

THE BURNING OF DARIEN sobered all the men of the Fifty-Fourth Massachusetts Infantry. Word quietly got around in the ranks: Colonel Shaw had vowed to never put the Fifty-Fourth under Colonel Montgomery's command for any more raids—not if he could help it. But even Danny knew that if Shaw was ordered to and refused, he could be court-martialed.

Back at their camp on St. Simons Island, Danny spent as much time as he could with Regent and the other horses. Taking care of horses was familiar; this he knew was honorable work. But as he brushed red mud out of Regent's sleek coat, he kept remembering the pile of charred buildings they'd left after the Second South Carolina was done looting and burning. Montgomery had ordered it, but what if God—

"Hey, Danny!"

Danny peered over Regent's broad back. Private Caldwell was coming toward the grove of trees where the line of officers' horses swished flies in the shade. "Everything all right? Didn't see you at the mess tent today."

Danny frowned, his mind still sorting thoughts. "Whose side is God on in this war, James?"

The young private blinked. "Why... the Union side, of course."

"So does that make what we did at Darien all right?"

James leaned on Regent's other side. "Well... no. The *cause* is just. But people are people; some good, some bad. On both sides, I suppose."

"Hmm." Danny worked his brush down Regent's legs. "You got a Bible, James?"

"Sure. Don't you?"

"Nah. But I'd like one if I could." Hadn't Frederick Douglass risked beatings to read the Bible for himself when he was Danny's age? Danny had been born free—but didn't take advantage of his freedom to read the Bible. It was about time.

"I'll get you one from the chaplain," James offered. "But I better go. Just heard we've been ordered back to South Carolina to support the coming assault on Charleston."

"Support?" Danny snorted. "What's that mean—digging more ditches?"

James wagged his head. "Huh. One of these days, they're gonna realize they need us to do some real fighting."

The Fifty-Fourth Massachusetts and the Second South Carolina were among the regiments who reported to General George Strong on June 25 at St. Helena Island, where Strong was gathering a force large enough to capture Morris Island and Fort Wagner at the mouth of Charleston Harbor. The Fifty-Fourth made camp near the beach on St. Helena, enjoying the sea breezes and a chance to cool off in the surf.

Danny got up before five o'clock roll call to take a swim, before there were too many eyes staring at his deformed foot. As he dove through the gentle waves and let the tide wash him back up on the nearly deserted beach one morning, Danny felt the same kind of freedom he felt on horseback. All he needed was his strong arms to pull him through the salty water. But once back on the sand, his speed was once more reduced to his quirky hop-step, hop-step.

As Danny pulled on his sandy trousers after his swim, he was startled by an unpleasant laugh behind him. "Well, if it ain't our ol' friend Turtle!" Danny whirled. Standing not five feet away, arms crossed, were Tom and Sam, his old tormentors from

Rochester, wearing the plain blue jacket and slouch hat of Union privates. Danny stared. He'd heard there were some New York regiments here on St. Helena Island, but he never thought—

"Who let you into the army?" Sam glared at him, as if Danny's presence somehow diminished his own importance.

"Why, Sam, we shouldn't be surprised." Tom's tone was mocking. "*Somebody* needs to do the dirty work so *real* soldiers can fight. Why do you think they raised a colored regiment, after all?"

Danny's eyes narrowed, and he clenched his fists so hard his fingernails dug into his flesh.

"Uh-oh, he's getting mad," taunted Tom. "We better run for our lives, Sam—oh! I forgot. Turtle can't run. Ha ha ha, heh heh..." Tom and Sam doubled over with laughter.

Danny was too angry to speak. He grabbed his shirt and shoes from the sand and limped away as fast as he could manage. He didn't even care if they laughed at his awkward gait. How *dare* those two rats insult his regiment—and all black soldiers, for that matter! Real soldiers? This war *was* going to be won by real soldiers—and not by the likes of those two, either, who didn't even realize they were supposed to be on the same side.

When Danny got back to the camp, Colonel Shaw was whistling in his wall tent as he shaved and didn't notice his orderly's sour face. "You don't need to saddle Regent this morning, Danny. It's payday! I'm going to muster the troops right after breakfast to give them their pay, then"—he wiped his grin with a towel—"I have a lot of paper work to do."

Payday? Had it really been a whole month since they left Boston? That would sweeten his sour morning. Danny stifled a snicker. "Paper work," on the other hand, could mean military reports—or writing to his bride, Annie, back in New York.

Right after breakfast, the officers of the Fifty-Fourth set up a couple supply boxes outside the quartermaster's tent and assembled the troops. None of the men had received any pay since the fifty dollars they got on enlisting—most of which had gone straight to their families back home. Spirits were high. Same pay as white soldiers—that's what they'd been promised. The first time in their lives they'd been paid on a scale equal to whites. "Man! I do love the army!" said a laughing voice as the men waited for the officers to get on with the roll call. Danny recognized John Wall, the handsome flag bearer from Oberlin, Ohio, who carried the Stars and Stripes. Wall and Henry Peal—who carried the Massachusetts flag—both grew up in Oberlin and had enlisted together.

What was taking so long? The officers kept frowning, putting their heads together, shuffling through papers. Shaw's cheerful mood had been replaced by a dark frown. But he finally gave the nod to go ahead.

Lieutenant Colonel Ned Hallowell began reading the roll call for Company A. He shoved some paper bills at the first man and said tersely, "Sign here." The man stared at the bills in his hand. "But there's only seven dollars here... sir."

The men within earshot of the makeshift desk looked at one another, and a murmur began to spread. Danny couldn't believe he'd heard right. He didn't know what his own pay would be—he didn't expect a soldier's pay—but he knew Lewis and Charles had been told thirteen dollars a month, just like all the other soldiers in the Union army.

Colonel Shaw stepped forward, hands clasped behind his back, his face muscles taut. "I am as disturbed as you are, private. But the requisition here"—he picked up a sheaf of papers—"says ten dollars per soldier *minus* three dollars for army issue clothing."

"Ten dollars!" "*Minus* three for our clothes?" "That's robbery!" Voices rose throughout all ten companies.

Shaw held up a gloved hand. Gradually the voices sank into a frustrated grumble. "I will look into the matter immediately," Shaw said. "But in the meantime, this is what we have." He looked at Hallowell. "Proceed."

But the private stepped back. "I won't take it—and I won't sign. Not until the U.S. Government gives us what it promised—the pay for a Union soldier. No more, no less."

"That's right!" The whole regiment began to shout. "We won't take it!"

Danny was shocked at the uproar. No pay meant no money for the families back home. Seven dollars was unfair—but at least it was *something*. He watched Shaw's face carefully. Would the colonel get angry at this rebellion? But Shaw's chin went up and Danny saw a glint in his eye that looked like... what? Pride. "So be it," he said. "The Fifty-Fourth will not accept its pay in protest for breach of contract." As the other officers gathered up the papers and sacks of bills, Shaw turned on his heel and strode off.

Colonel Shaw sent off a sharply worded letter to Governor Andrew about the pay fiasco. But the blatant discrimination took another shape. By July 3, General Strong had moved most of the white regiments from St. Helena to islands surrounding Charleston to prepare for an assault on Fort Wagner. But the black regiments had been left behind to "guard the camps." Inactivity was the men's worst enemy.

Danny's feelings were mixed. Good riddance to Tom and Sam, anyway. But he knew Shaw was bitterly disappointed. So when the order came by ship five days later for the remaining regiments on St. Helena to get on board and join General Strong's force "immediately," he worked feverishly to help load the horses. The order had been crisp: "Take only blankets, cold rations, and battle equipment."

This was it.

Steaming up the Stono River, the Fifty-Fourth—minus two companies that had been left behind to guard the camp—unloaded on James Island in plain view of Confederate sentries on nearby hills. Their objective: to create a diversion from an even larger Union force preparing to capture Morris Island and Fort Wagner.

But it was "hurry up and wait." News of Confederate defeats at Gettysburg, Pennsylvania, and Vicksburg in Mississippi—along with staggering casualties on both sides—boosted Union confidence. Then came word: The "surprise" attack by General Strong had only gained a foothold on the southern end of Morris Island. Fort Wagner, with its huge earthen walls and big guns, still straddled the narrow neck at the north end of the island, protected by the sea on one side and a marshy river on the other.

With pockets of Confederate soldiers all over James Island, both white and black troops served sentry duty. The night of July 15, Shaw put four companies of his men on a picket line, along with the Tenth Connecticut—a white regiment. Studying the situation, Shaw told his officers gravely, "The Tenth has their backsides against a swamp. If we get attacked tonight, it'll be up to the Fifty-Fourth to hold the line, or they're goners." And to Danny he said tersely, "Leave Regent saddled tonight."

Danny turned to go, but Colonel Shaw called him back. "And Danny, if anything happens to me, make sure my horse gets back to my wife, Annie. Promise?"

Bedding down near the horses, Danny tossed and

turned. His stomach rumbled—rations were down to hard bread and water. Why did Colonel Shaw make him promise to return his horse to his wife? Surely nothing would happen to the colonel...

The attack came at dawn. Danny awakened with a start as Colonel Shaw yelled, "My horse, Danny!" In a moment, the tie was undone and Shaw vaulted into the saddle with his sword drawn. "Fall in! Fall in!" he yelled to the rest of the regiment, heading for the picket line, which was standing fast, guns to shoulders, returning fire as yelling bands of Confederates tried to divide the line and isolate the Tenth Connecticut. Moving the relief horses farther back behind the lines, Danny could see flashes of fire and clouds of smoke popping from every clump of bushes; small cannons boomed from surrounding hills. Men began to fall; other men moved into the gaps. Soon it was hand-to-hand combat.

Heart in his mouth, Danny held tight to the halter ropes of the skittish horses as gunfire came from right and left. Hold tight... hold tight. That's all he had to do.

The Battle of James Island was on.

The fierce resistance of the Fifty-Fourth held the line long enough for the Tenth Connecticut to escape their death trap and gave time for the rest of the regiments to make a line of battle. Artillery support from the gun ships in the Sono River finally allowed

the Union troops to advance—and the Rebels with-
drew as suddenly as they had appeared.

Silence settled like a suffocating blanket on the battlefield—broken suddenly by a cheer. "Hooray for the Fifty-Fourth!" "You saved our hides, Fifty-Fourth!" "Give 'em a cheer, boys!" Hearing the shouts, Danny left the horses to see what was happening. To his astonishment, the white soldiers of the Tenth Connecticut were tossing their caps in the air in a show of support for the Fifty-Fourth Massachusetts. Soon other white regiments were joining the cheers.

Danny knew Colonel Shaw must feel gratified that his men had been tested—and had proven themselves, just as he knew they would. But Shaw held up his gloved hand to quiet the troops, dismounted, and began to walk among the fallen, searching for the wounded. Drawn by a sober curiosity, Danny followed. In death, blue and gray lay together as brothers. Blood mingled with blood. When the wounded had been located and moved to the surgeon's tent, the grim task of burying the dead began.

Grabbing a shovel, Danny worked alongside Shaw, hoping against hope he would not discover Charles or Lewis, or James Caldwell for that matter, among the dead. Coming around a bush, Danny nearly stumbled over a small figure clad in a Confederate uniform, rifle at his side. Blood drenched the front of the gray uniform, but the face was smooth and childlike—barely older than Danny himself, if that. Danny just stared. This boy, so like himself, would never grow up into manhood. Did he like horses? Grits and biscuits?...

Several other men from the Fifty-Fourth stopped to see the child-soldier. With special tenderness, they dug a grave and laid the youngster gently within, hands folded respectfully on his blood-soaked chest. "I hope it wasn't my bullet that killed him," muttered one of the gravediggers.

As the long, weary day came to an end, Colonel Shaw ordered roll call to determine the number of casualties in his regiment. With a start, Danny noticed that Private James Caldwell did not answer when his name was called. He was not among the dead or wounded. That meant he was "missing." Had he been captured? Rumors of black prisoners being bayoneted or even sold as slaves shook Danny to the core.

He wanted to sink to the ground, head in his hands. But he tried to get a grip on himself. He was part of the army; he had a job to do. The horses needed rubbing down, feed, and water. Regent had yet to be unsaddled....

With sudden horror, Danny looked about wildly. Regent! Where was Regent? He had seen Colonel Shaw dismount before scouting out the dead and wounded on foot. But where had Regent gone?

Running to where the relief horses had been picketed, he hoped against hope that Regent had wandered back to his companions and was waiting patiently to be rid of his saddle and bridle.

But the chestnut horse was not there.

Colonel Shaw's prize horse was missing.

Chapter 10

Inside the Fort

*D*ON'T PANIC, DANNY TOLD HIMSELF. *Regent probably just wandered off a short way and is filling his belly with marsh grass.* If he found the horse soon, no one would ever need to know Regent had gone missing.

First thing to do: check all the camps behind the sentry lines. Shouldn't be hard. Most of the tents, except for the battlefield surgery tent and a few for the officers, had been left behind on St. Helena. Keeping eyes alert for the familiar chestnut hide, Danny walked as quickly as his clubfoot allowed, avoiding the small groups of soldiers gathering around supper fires. But here and there he picked

up snatches of conversation: "Fifty-Fourth did all right today."... "More than all right! Saved our hides."... "Heard we're heading for Morris Island tonight."... "What? Storm's coming in soon."

They were moving out tonight? He *had* to find Regent! But it didn't take long to reach a dismal conclusion: Regent was nowhere to be found in the camps.

Pushing his awkward hop-step, hop-step almost to a run, Danny headed away from the camps, past the freshly dug graves, and into the unknown forests and marshlands that made up James Island. Did he dare call out Regent's name? He decided against it. He didn't want to announce to the whole Union army that he'd lost Colonel Shaw's horse... and he sure didn't want to announce his presence to any stray Rebel soldiers out there.

Dark clouds rolling in from the sea plunged the island into a premature dusk. Rumbling thunder and occasional flashes of lightning signaled the coming storm. Behind him, the campfires were winking out, one by one. He tried to think. If Regent hadn't wandered back into the camp, which way would he go? Not toward the marsh—a horse likes to keep its feet on solid ground. Danny headed away from the marsh. He had to hurry or the Fifty-Fourth and the other regiments would leave without him—

Danny shook that thought out of his head and pushed forward. From time to time, he stopped and listened... nothing. His clubfoot was beginning to feel the strain of the search, sending echoes of pain all the way up his leg. Should he go back? His mind and body were sorely tempted… but his will screamed, *No!* He couldn't go back without Regent. Not yet, anyway.

Danny tried to focus his mind on the path, but it seemed to have disappeared. The ground squished beneath his shoes. Suddenly Danny tripped over a root and pitched off the squishy path, landing in six inches of stinking water. Muddy and wet, he scrambled to his feet. This was crazy. He would never find Regent in this—

Wait. What was that? He stood stock-still and listened again. Somewhere to his right he heard a snuffling noise, the kind a horse makes when it's drinking water. Could it be—? Creeping forward, he edged toward the sound. Straining his eyes, he tried to sort out the dark shapes around him. Then—suddenly—a bright flash of lightning lit up the shadows, for one brief moment sorting them into trees… bushes… and Regent, standing ankle deep in marshy water, looking lost and miserable.

Nearly delirious with joy, Danny waded toward his prize, murmuring, "Easy boy, easy"—but just as he grabbed the trailing reins, a clap of thunder startled the horse and it jumped back, pulling Danny down into the marshy water again.

But he hung on.

Scrambling to his feet and quieting the trembling horse, Danny hauled himself, muddy and wet, into the saddle. He was so happy at finding Regent he wanted to shout. But he had a pressing problem to solve before he could celebrate: Which way back to camp?

A steady rain began to fall as Danny tried to guide Regent out of the shallow marsh. At one point, the pair stumbled onto what looked like a road—but which way to go? Danny hated to admit it, but he was hopelessly lost. Horse and boy stood uncertainly on the road as Danny tried to think, rain dripping down his collar. He felt, more than saw, Regent's head swing to the left as though toward a sound. Danny strained his ears. He heard the sound, too—like the squeak of wagon wheels and plodding hoofbeats coming his way. That did it. He had to go right. But just as he pulled right on the reins and kicked with his right heel, he heard another sound—coming from the right. Voices. More horses. A short laugh.

Pulling up short, Danny felt caught in a vise, squeezing tighter from both sides. With only seconds to act, he slid off Regent's back, quickly loosened the cinch under the horse's belly, and pulled off the saddle and blanket with its U.S. markings. Stripping off his Union jacket, canteen, and cap, he plunged back into the marsh and stuck saddle and clothes behind the largest bunch of reeds he could find. He no sooner got back on to the road when the first of his fellow travelers loomed out of the dreary night: two mules pulling a creaky old wagon, driven by an older man with skin black as ink.

"Whoooa." The old man pulled up beside Danny and with a shrewd glance sized up horse and boy, both muddy and tense. "Git up on this wagon, boy," he ordered.

"My horse—"

"Yer horse, nothin'!" hissed the man. "Turn it loose—now!" He jerked his chin toward the growing sound of voices and hoofbeats coming toward them.

Danny hesitated. He couldn't lose Regent again! But with surprising agility, the man leaned over, grabbed the reins out of Danny's hand, and smacked Regent on the rump with the long willow switch he had in his hands. With a surprised snort, Regent took off down the road to the left, going the direction the wagon had just come from.

A howl of protest rose in Danny's chest—but just then five horses and riders appeared out of the wet gloom. Rebel soldiers! He swallowed his cry.

"What you doin' out here on the road, boy!" challenged one of the riders. Danny thought *he* was being addressed, but as the rider came closer—dressed in the gray uniform of a Confederate sergeant—he realized the Rebel soldier was talking to the old man. "Was there someone else with you? We heard a horse a moment ago."

The old man scratched his head, as if he couldn't think fast. "Nah. Thunder scared our nag tied to the back o' the wagon—took off. Boy tried ta grab 'im, but—" The old man shrugged. "Reckon he'll git on back home."

"What are you doin' out on the road tonight? Do you have orders?"

"Oh, yessuh!" The old man jerked a thumb toward the back of the wagon. "Deliverin' these here water barrels ta Fort Wagner."

Danny stood motionless in the road. Confederate cavalry? An old man delivering water barrels to Fort Wagner? What had he gotten himself into?

Just then another Confederate soldier rode up close to the wagon. "It's Unc Calhoun, sergeant. I've seen him come to the fort before. Regular delivery."

The sergeant seemed to consider as his horse tossed its head impatiently. "Mud's gonna get worse before this storm lets up," he grunted. "We'll give you an escort, make sure this wagon gets to the fort and not into the hands of those blasted Yankees."

As the Confederate sergeant waved two of his mounted soldiers to bring up the rear behind the wagon, Unc Calhoun glared at Danny. "Didn' Ah tell you ta git back in the wagon, boy?" he hollered. "Yo' mama gonna have mah hide if Ah lose you in th' swamp."

Danny scrambled into the back of the wagon, his insides churning. Somewhere out there Regent was lost... again. Why did the old man chase him away? But deep down, Danny knew why. No one in the world—and especially not a squad of Confederate soldiers—would believe a clubfooted boy like him was the owner of a beautiful piece of horseflesh like Regent. And somehow—thanks to the old man—the Confederate soldiers didn't seem to suspect he was attached to the Union army, or he might be a prisoner right now instead of Unc Calhoun's "boy."

Although, what difference did it make? He was headed straight into the Confederate stronghold with not one idea how he was going to get out again.

Danny had not realized how exhausted he was until he got on the wagon. When he awoke hours later—his foot and ankle throbbing, neck muscles stiff from leaning against the water barrels, his clothes soaked from the steady rain—night had already lifted, though still under leaden skies, and the wagon stood ready, along with several other supply wagons, to drive onto a flatboat ferry.

"Git up here, boy, an' help me with these mules," ordered the old man loudly, with a slight brush of his finger to his lips. Danny caught the signal to keep his mouth shut.

When it was their turn to load, Danny took the halter of the lead mule and coaxed the big animals up the planks onto the deck of the ferry. Working as quickly as his sore muscles allowed, he snapped tie ropes to the halters and made sure they were tied securely to the gunwales of the old ferry, which sorely needed a paint job. As the paddlewheel along one side began to turn, fired by an ancient steam engine, Danny noticed that their "escorts" had not boarded and were riding back the way they had come. Must be a patrol for James Island, he thought.

As the ferry came around a small island in the middle of the river that divided James Island from Morris Island, their destination loomed before them. Fort Wagner, its massive earthen walls straddling the narrow neck at the north end of Morris Island, looked huge and indestructible. Unc Calhoun joined him and leaned in close to his ear. "Where you from, boy? Tell me quick; we ain't got much time."

Danny hesitated. This old man worked for the Confederates! But... he'd also saved his hide last night. He decided to trust him, quickly identifying himself as an orderly for Colonel Robert Shaw, commander of the Fifty-Fourth Massachusetts, a regiment of free blacks. "Colonel's horse ran off after the battle yesterday," Danny admitted. "I had just found him when you found me."

The old man's eyes glittered. "Regiment o' free blacks, you say? Headin' fo' Fort Wagner?" The idea seemed to wash years from the man's tired face. "But jist lissen to you—talkin' like them Yankees. Keep yo' mouth shut an' let me do all the talkin', y'hear?" He was, he told Danny, a freedman who'd been pressed into service to deliver fresh water to the fort on a weekly basis. Southern blacks unwilling to aid the Confederate army were considered guilty of insurrection—"an' Ah don't aim to spend this war in some prison somewhere! We'll jist unload these barrels and get our hides outta there."

It couldn't happen soon enough for Danny. As the wagon rolled off the ferry and lumbered toward the huge walls, his heart began to pound and his breath came in short gasps. Unc Calhoun gave him a quick look. "Calm yo'self down, boy. Don't let nobody see you afraid. In fact, don't call no attention to yo'self nohow!"

But once inside the gates, even Unc Calhoun began to look worried. Everywhere they looked, Rebel soldiers were digging "bombproofs" and covering them with timber and sandbags. Trying to seem unconcerned, the old man and boy unloaded the heavy water barrels to their usual place—then were ordered to load them up again and move them to a more secure location in one of the bombproofs.

When they were finally done with the job, light was rapidly fading under the heavy cloud cover, though the rain had stopped. Unc Calhoun reported to the fort's quartermaster and made to leave. But as the empty wagon rattled toward the north gate, a guard stopped them. "Sorry, Uncle. Gate's been locked. No one goes in or out anymore tonight."

"But—" Now even Unc Calhoun looked alarmed.

The Confederate guard waved impatiently. "Do as you're told, old man! Yankee army's got the whole south end of the island, and they're hunkering down just a half mile away. You'll be safer inside the fort."

Reluctantly, Unc Calhoun turned the mules. Danny's fingers gripped the wagon seat until his knuckles ached. The Union army had captured the south end of Morris Island and was preparing an assault on the fort! The men of the Fifty-Fourth had talked of little else, wanting to be part of the action, unlocking this first "key" to Charleston. It should have been exciting news, except for one thing:

Danny was trapped inside.

Chapter 11

One Gallant Rush

DANNY AND UNC CALHOUN SLEPT FITFULLY the night of July 17 in the bed of the wagon. The mules had been unharnessed and corralled in one of the bombproofs. Danny's stomach cramped with hunger and his clothes were still damp in the muggy South Carolina heat, but that wasn't the reason he shivered all night. Half awake, he could hear some of the Rebel soldiers talking as they worked through the night on the bombproofs.

"Yankee army's got a darkie regiment out there who think they're soldiers—ha!" There was general laughter.

"The white officers are to blame," snorted another. "Traitors to the

112

white race, that's what they are."

"Since they love the darkies so much, we'll dig a mass grave and let them rot together!" vowed another. A chorus of agreement greeted this last threat.

Sick at heart, Danny tried to picture the Fifty-Fourth, gathering just a half mile away on the beach along with the rest of the Union brigades preparing to bring Fort Wagner down. No one knew where he was—what if they thought he'd deserted? Or worse—that he'd stolen Colonel Shaw's horse!

The confidence he'd felt when Frederick Douglass brought him to Camp Meigs sank to the bottom of his spirit. He was nothing but a failure, after all. He'd lost Colonel Shaw's horse... got himself caught by the Rebels... might even get himself killed by the Union army! Hot tears of self-pity slid down his face, mingling with dried mud from his night in the marsh. But finally he slept.

Waking in the early hours of July 18, Danny sat up in the wagon bed and looked around cautiously. What were his chances for escape? Confederate guards, rifles at the ready, patrolled the top of the wide earthen walls. No hope there. He eyed the gates. Maybe they'd open the north gate this morning and he and Unc Calhoun could just drive out.

But in the next moment, Danny's hopes were smashed by a high whistle in the air above him and—*baroom!*—a loud explosion as a heavy shell slammed into the walls of Fort Wagner. The first explosion was followed by another and another. "Get in the bombproof! Get in the bombproof!" yelled a Rebel soldier, practically dragging Danny and Unc Calhoun into the nearest protection.

The bombardment was underway, led by big gunboats like the *New Ironsides* that had been gathering offshore for weeks. Union batteries to the south also lobbed shells at the fort as the fort's cannons responded in kind. *Baroom! Crash! Eeeeeeeee-boom!*

Time is a funny thing under extreme stress. A few seconds of silence seemed like an eternity, raising hopes that the latest explosion was the last one. Then another eerie whistle, followed by a huge blast and dirt raining down on their heads beneath the bombproof. And another. And another.

Danny huddled on the floor of the bombproof next to Unc Calhoun, his head tucked into his arm to protect his face from the raining debris. A wounded soldier was brought in and laid at their feet; a replacement ran out to take over the cannon he'd been firing. Shoulders hunched, Danny stared at the man's bloody face and shattered shoulder. It hit him like a thunderbolt: People were going to die here today! Was he going to be one of them? *Oh God, Oh God!* He wasn't used to praying, except before meals and in church. But only God knew he was inside the fort, being shot at by his own army. He tried to remember what he'd been reading in the Bible James Caldwell got for him, but all he could think of was the familiar psalm Grammy used to say when she tucked him in at night: "The Lord is my shepherd, I shall not want. He makes me to lie down in green pastures—"

Eeeeeee-boom! Crash!... Varoom! Crash!

How many hours had passed? Danny had no idea, except that the sun in the hazy sky hung low in the west when the bombs stopped. Taking a peek outside, Danny was surprised to see no one on the walls. Had the Rebels surrendered? He moved closer to the doorway of the bombproof where he could see more of the fort. Soldiers by the hundreds still milled about inside, carrying the wounded into the bombproofs, reloading weapons, whittling sharp stakes, moving quickly and quietly. Lying in a row were the Confederate dead. Danny counted... six, seven, eight. Only *eight*?

"Hey, old man!" Speaking in a low voice, a guard waved Unc Calhoun out of the bombproof. Danny followed at his heels. "Harness up your mules and help these men load the dead into your wagon. Be quick about it—and no talking."

Unc Calhoun's eyes quickly took in the situation, pressed his lips into a tight line, and headed for the mules. As he and Danny backed the mules into the traces, the old man whispered, "It be a trap. They wants them Yanks to think th' bombing ha' weakened they defenses so they send in th' ground troops. But it be a bloodbath fo' sure."

Danny felt weak in the knees. Ground troops.

That meant the first Union soldiers who came over that wall would be dead meat. Who would General Strong send in as the frontal assault? But even as his mind asked the question, Danny's guts knew the answer: the Fifty-Fourth. They wouldn't have to be ordered; Shaw would volunteer if given half a chance. Even with the good showing at the battle on James Island, the Fifty-Fourth had a lot to prove to a skeptical nation, and they were willing to die proving it.

The feeling of helplessness made Danny want to scream. He was inside the fort. He knew it was a trap. And there wasn't a thing he could do about it.

Darkness began to settle over the fort, intensifying the silence. What was happening outside? Then, floating on the sea breezes, came the sound of singing, low and soulful. Danny stifled a bitter laugh. Only the Fifty-Fourth could sing like that.

Lookouts posted near the gun ports inside the fort suddenly passed silent signals; quickly and quietly, hundreds of Confederates took up positions inside the walls—but not on top. Cannon fire once more whistled overhead, doing little damage to the double-thick walls—but the guns of Fort Wagner remained silent.

And then the cannons stopped. Danny strained his ears. Did he hear the tramp of running feet outside? At another signal, hundreds of Rebels suddenly swarmed onto the top of the walls and began firing. No sooner had one soldier fired and dropped behind the wall to reload than another took his place—and another. They fired in waves, pointing

their rifles straight down.

The Union troops must be trying to cross the stake-studded moat around the fort and scale the walls!

Suddenly Danny began to run for the walls as fast

as he could with his awkward gait. "Danny! Come back!" He heard Unc Calhoun call his name, but the old man didn't understand. If that was the Fifty-Fourth on the other side of those walls, that's where Danny belonged!

Ignored by the Rebel soldiers, Danny scrambled past them, up the "steps" dug into the earthen walls, along the ledges halfway up. He had to get to the top! He had to see—

Suddenly Danny heard a familiar voice above him. "Forward, brave men! Forward!" Colonel Shaw's voice. It *was* the Fifty-Fourth! Jerking his head back, Danny saw Colonel Shaw gain the top of the wall, with Sergeant Major Lewis Douglass right beside him. "Rally! Rally!" cried Shaw, sword raised high, as other blue uniforms gained the top and immediately engaged in hand-to-hand fighting with the Rebel soldiers.

But no sooner did that cry leave his mouth than a bullet crashed into Shaw's chest. In horror, Danny saw the Fifty-Fourth's commander pitch headfirst over the wall and land on the floor of the fort below.

For a moment, time seemed to stand still in Danny's head. Shouts, rifle fire, the screams of the wounded, confusion, and commotion roared around him, but it all seemed muted and far away. But only for a moment. Suddenly, below, inside the fort, he saw half a dozen soldiers from the Fifty-Fourth taking a valiant stand around Shaw's body. Looking up, he saw Lewis Douglass taking charge, shouting commands, using his rifle butt, his bayonet, even his boots to beat back the Rebels from the top of the wall.

Something else caught Danny's eye above him— the state flag of Massachusetts, tattered almost to shreds, waving defiantly. Corporal Henry Peal plunged the staff into the top and held on tight, even as an enraged Confederate soldier grabbed hold of the flag and ripped it off its staff.

Where was the Stars and Stripes? Without thinking, Danny scrambled the last few feet up to the top of the wall and looked down. What he saw made him gasp in horror. Bodies in Union blue lay sprawled on the sloping outside walls of the fort, some crying out in pain, others still in death. More bodies in the moat below. But still more members of the Fifty-Fourth kept coming. And there—the Stars and Stripes, nearing the top of the sloping walls. Danny reached out a hand and pulled—but it was not John Wall holding the flag aloft but Sergeant William Carney. Gaining the top, Carney plunged the staff into the earth beside the empty staff that Corporal Peal still gripped proudly.

Danny realized it was now or never. To stay with Unc Calhoun was to risk capture as a prisoner of war. He hurled himself over the edge and flattened himself, facedown, against the outside of the wall. He lay still as bullets and yells filled the air around him.

How long could the Fifty-Fourth hold out? They were outnumbered three times over by the Rebels inside the fort. Finally through the mayhem he heard

Sergeant Major Douglass yell, "Retreat, men! Retreat!"

Back down the wall they came. Danny slid and scrambled for his life as bullets hit the ground around him on every side. *Help me, Jesus! Help me!* He stumbled over a body and realized it was John Wall, dead. Then, out of the corner of his eye, he saw Carney go down, shot in the leg. Incredibly, Carney still held the Stars and Stripes aloft. Danny scrambled over to the young sergeant and helped him to his feet, wrapping an arm around his waist. Wincing in pain, Carney gave him a lopsided grin. "Hey, Danny. Where you come from?"

Together, Danny and Sergeant Carney struggled through the moat with its wicked spiked stakes and crawled out the other side. The flag was in tatters but still flew from its staff. Then, with a cry, Carney pitched forward again. Danny caught him and saw that Carney was bleeding from a bullet wound to the head. "Can't... let 'er touch... the ground," the soldier gasped.

Stumbling, half-crawling, Danny dragged Carney back down the narrow neck of land between ocean and marsh to the Union lines. They had to stand in the surf as the Tenth Connecticut trotted past them at quick time to relieve the Fifty-Fourth.

Hands reached out as Danny and Sergeant Carney stumbled behind Union lines. "It never touched... the ground, boys!" Carney croaked, giving up the flag to other hands. Collapsing on the sand, Danny watched in shocked silence as what was left of the Fifty-Fourth straggled in. Behind them, the sound of battle continued, now in the hands of other regiments struggling to mount the forbidding walls of Fort Wagner.

The last of the Fifty-Fourth to come was Sergeant Major Douglass, who gave Danny a strange look as he passed. Then he turned to look back at the fort and Danny knew what he was thinking:

They had to go back for their dead and wounded.

Chapter 12

Lost and Found

A<small>T MIDNIGHT, ALL FIRING CEASED.</small> The Union field hospital tent behind the sand dunes was filled with the wounded and dying—but dozens more lay strewn on the battlefield. Under cover of darkness, men crawled back toward the fort, trying to locate the dead and the wounded.

Limping badly, Danny wandered about the makeshift camp, dazed and exhausted. Who was in charge? Colonel Shaw was dead... Lieutenant Colonel Hallowell lay in the hospital tent, wounded in the groin... even General Strong was missing and presumed dead! As the Union regiments tried to assess their losses during the night, the men of the Fifty-Fourth gathered in ragged companies, shrunken almost by half. In shock, they realized that so many of their officers had been killed, wounded, or captured that Captain Emilio—ninth in command and only nineteen years old—was the senior officer!

As soon as dawn broke the darkness, the Union army sent a flag of truce to the fort, asking permission to retrieve their remaining dead and wounded. But the messenger returned with bitter news: Their request had been refused. "The Rebs say they have plenty of doctors to tend the wounded, who are now their prisoners. And plenty of soldiers"—the messenger's voice cracked—"to bury the 'Yankee dead.'"

Frustration and anger spread among the remaining soldiers of the Fifty-Fourth. The rules of war required both North and South to bury the dead and treat the wounded and captured with respect. But the Confederates had made it clear they had no intention to treat "nigger soldiers" with the same respect. And the Confederate Congress had extended these harsh repercussions to white officers of black regiments: All officers leading black troops (said the Confederate proclamation) were guilty of "inciting slave insurrection" and, if captured, would be put to death or otherwise severely punished.

Danny hunkered down near Sergeant Major Douglass as the men mourned their losses, trying to ignore his aching belly. Both water and food were critically short until relief supplies arrived, and what they had was needed for the wounded. But in spite of his exhaustion, Danny was engulfed by the intense emotion of the men. Many wept. They had fought so hard, so bravely—the other Union regiments on Morris Island were calling the charge of the Fifty-Fourth "Splendid! Gallantly fought!"—but at what cost? The fort had not been taken. Their own colonel, leading the charge, was dead. What would happen to their wounded? *Their* colonel's body?

Without thinking, Danny plucked on Lewis Douglass's sleeve. "They said they're gonna dump the colonel's body in a mass grave with the other dead."

The sergeant major's eyes narrowed, as if seeing the boy for the first time. "What do you mean, 'they said'?" he snapped. "How do *you* know what they said?" His hand shot out and grabbed Danny by the front of his shirt, jerking him to his feet. "Come to think of it, you went missing after the battle on James Island. Where have you been? Where is your uniform? How do you know what the Rebs are saying?"

Stuttering badly, Danny blurted out his desperate search for Colonel Shaw's horse, finding him, then having to let him go when the Rebel patrol caught him on the road. He told how Unc Calhoun had covered for him, made the Rebs think he was helping to deliver the water barrels to the fort... which is why he ended up *inside* Fort Wagner.

Trembling, Danny waited for angry words to tell him what a fool he was, worthless, no good... but it didn't come. Instead, Lewis Douglass released his

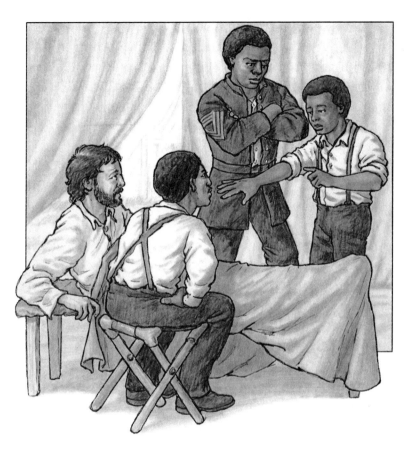

hold on the boy's shirt, took his arm, and marched him to where Captain Emilio was conferring with the wounded Hallowell.

"This boy was inside the fort," Lewis announced. "Danny Sims, Colonel Shaw's orderly. Maybe he needs to be debriefed."

Lieutenant Colonel Hallowell leaned up on his elbow, wincing in pain. "Inside the fort? How—"

Once more Danny had to tell his story, humiliated

at having to admit he'd found the colonel's horse only to lose him again. But Hallowell and Emilio didn't seem interested in the horse. They asked question after question: How many men were in the fort? Why had the guns gone silent before the charge? How had they survived eleven hours of shelling from the gunboats? Bombproofs? How many?

Finally the questions ceased. "You may go," Hallowell muttered, sinking back on the cot. The interview had obviously exhausted him. But as Danny left the hospital tent, he saw the wounded officer glance at him, then say something to Emilio and Douglass.

Danny didn't know what to do. Were they angry that he'd known about the trap and hadn't warned them? That he'd lost Colonel Shaw's horse? He didn't know what else he could have done... but he knew he'd failed miserably. Jamming his hands into his trouser pockets, he limped slowly through the camp. His foot and leg were aching so badly after the mad dash getting away from the fort that he had to fight back tears. His hop-step, hop-step gait got steadily worse.

Ending up on the beach, Danny threw himself down on the sand under some wild scrub bushes. He'd joined the Fifty-Fourth as Colonel Shaw's orderly. Now Shaw was dead and Regent... gone. He didn't have his Union jacket and cap or his canteen anymore. Would they give him another uniform? Probably not. He was just in the way now....

Exhausted, Danny slept as the July sun marched

west behind the sand dunes, casting long shadows on the ocean side of Morris Island. When he awoke, he at first couldn't remember where he was. Why was he lying on the ground, his mouth full of gritty sand? He had a wrenching feeling in his gut, like... like something was terribly wrong. Or maybe he was just terribly hungry. He tried to swallow, but his mouth was dry, his lips cracked. Water. He had to get some water.

He sat up. Dusk had fallen, and it would soon be fully dark. As the waves licked his battered shoes at high tide, it all came back: the lost horse, the battle at Fort Wagner, Colonel Shaw... dead. But Danny's hunger and thirst were desperate now. He'd better go back to where the Fifty-Fourth was camped—though he dreaded showing up again, like a discarded shoe that people kept around just in case its mate showed up.

Wait— He heard the creak of a wagon and hoofbeats coming from the south, nearly muffled in the sand. Danny struggled to his feet. Maybe he could get a ride the few hundred yards back to Union lines. Pulling himself up to the beaten track, Danny squinted into the darkness. Mules... a supply wagon. And tied to the back was a sorry-looking horse, mane tangled and matted, coat muddied, head hanging—

"Regent!" he croaked. "Stop! Stop!"

The driver of the wagon hauled back on his reins, peering through the dusk at Danny. "Who are you, boy? You know this horse?"

"Yes, sir!" Danny licked his dry lips. "I'm... I'm

Colonel Shaw's orderly—Fifty-Fourth Massachusetts Infantry. This is Colonel Shaw's horse—got lost on James Island."

The supply wagon driver looked at his partner, then back at Danny. "That's where we found this horse. Didn't seem to belong to nobody, so we just brought him along when we ferried across." He jerked a thumb. "Go on, climb in back. We'll check out your story with Colonel Shaw."

Danny winced. "Colonel Shaw is dead... sir. But the Fifty-Fourth is just up ahead. They can tell you."

With difficulty, Danny climbed into the back of the supply wagon. Regent raised his muddy head and gave a soft nicker. Danny's spirit rose a notch, his weariness, hunger, and thirst temporarily forgotten. Regent had been found. Regent recognized him.

The supply wagon with its barrels of water and sacks of hardtack and dried meat was a welcome sight. Sergeant Major Lewis Douglass identified the horse, which was turned over to Danny with little comment. A lost—and found—horse was the least of the concerns facing the regiment, because the supply wagon also brought disturbing news.

Earlier that week, the names of the first draftees had been printed in the New York papers. Outraged at being drafted into "Lincoln's emancipation war," which would probably cost them jobs when the freed slaves came north, and angry that the draft exempted anyone with three hundred dollars to pay a substitute, New York's Irish had taken to the streets in protest. The protest had turned ugly, turning its rage on the city's black residents as the "cause" of the problem. Homes were burned, a black orphanage attacked, families chased through the streets and pelted with sticks, rocks, and bricks.

"Got a message for..." The wagon driver dug a paper out of his pocket and peered at it in the flickering light from a nearby campfire. "...Sergeant Robert Simmons."

Lewis Douglass flinched. "Sergeant Simmons is missing. We don't know his fate." Douglass held out his hand for the message and scanned it. His face hardened. "On July 16, rioters attacked Simmons's sister and her two children. His—" Lewis's voice faltered. "His handicapped seven-year-old nephew was beaten to death by a mob."

Danny felt the blood drain from his face. The little boy was handicapped?—maybe crippled, like him, couldn't run away. "Maybe just as well Sergeant Simmons isn't here to get that message," he muttered. On July 16, Simmons had been fighting on James Island for respect, freedom, and the Union.

News of the riot upset the whole regiment. But they were Union soldiers now. They had a duty to perform. But a voice whispered inside Danny's head, *What is your duty?*

With a little water and food in his belly, the gears of Danny's mind began cranking again. Regent was back; Shaw was dead. Colonel Shaw had told Danny that if anything happened to him, to see that his horse got returned to his young wife. And Danny had promised.

His thoughts churned as he watered and fed Regent, then began to brush the dried mud out of the chestnut coat. His knapsack—had it come with the Fifty-Fourth when they did the night march from James Island over to Morris? It held all his earthly possessions—including the Bible James had given him. He was going to need that Bible.

By the time he finished caring for Regent, Danny had made up his mind. But he wasn't going to just disappear again. Searching through the camp, he found his knapsack in a pile along with Colonel Shaw's belongings. Feeling around inside, Danny's fingers closed on the Bible. Good.

New energy spurred his hop-step, hop-step gait into the hospital tent. Coming alongside one of the cots, he cleared his throat. "Lieutenant Colonel?"

Ned Hallowell's eyes opened. He looked feverish. But he gave a brief nod of recognition.

"Sir, Colonel Shaw's horse has been found. But the colonel made me promise that... that if anything happened to him, I would see that the horse got returned to his wife. I—I would like permission to do that, sir. Now."

Hallowell studied him. "Annie Shaw lives in New York City." The unspoken question hung in the air. *Didn't you hear that New York just had the worst race riot in history?*

Danny swallowed. "I know, sir." He stuck his chin in the air. "I promised, sir."

A trace of a smile flickered on the wounded officer's face. "Permission granted."

Chapter 13

The Long Road Home

With written permission in his knapsack from Captain Emilio to get him on a Union supply ship, Danny hunted up Lewis and Charles Douglass to say good-bye. Lewis didn't say much, just shook his hand and handed him a letter. "Give this to my father when you see him."

Charles was more practical. "Here," he said, thrusting out a uniform jacket and cap. "James Caldwell was about your size. I think he'd want you to have 'em." He handed Danny his own haversack of food and a canteen. "You're goin' to need this."

Danny hesitated, but the question burned in his mouth. "Where's the Fifty-Fourth going to go now?"

Lewis Douglass tipped up his chin resolutely. "Go? We're not going anywhere. We have a job to finish."

A thin sliver of new moon hung in the midnight sky, barely lighting the hulk of Fort Wagner behind him as Danny and Regent set out for the south end of Morris Island. He was sorry about losing Colonel Shaw's saddle... but Regent's bare back felt good beneath his legs. Just like old times when he exercised Wendell or William along the river road back in Rochester. Except back in Rochester, all he had to worry about was running into Tom and Sam's jeers and taunts—not treacherous marshes or Confederate patrols.

But the south end of Morris Island had been secured by the Union army, and sunrise found Danny and Regent waiting for low tide at Lighthouse Inlet so they could swim across to Folly Island, the long narrow island that shielded James Island from the sea. "But at some point we have to get over to the far side of James Island along the Sono River," Danny worried aloud to Regent. That was where the Union ships unloaded troops and supplies and therefore was his only hope for gaining passage back to New York. But between here and there, Danny had to retrace the nightmare march the Fifty-Fourth had taken after the battle on James Island.

"I'll take it easy," Danny promised Regent, smoothing the milky forelock as the horse nibbled on one of his uniform buttons. "Wanna get you back home in good shape."

The trip to the Sono River took two days and two nights. Danny slept three to four hours as best he could, then pushed on for several hours. Every step of the way was guided by three things: avoiding Confederate patrols, finding fresh water for Regent and himself, and not exhausting his horse. "Gonna get you home in good shape," Danny murmured as they picked their way through numerous creeks and marshes dotting the islands.

Staying on constant alert for Rebel patrols didn't give Danny much thinking time, but the "Battle Hymn" that had taken over the tune to "John Brown's Body" played again and again in his mind. *Mine eyes have seen the glory of the coming of the Lord... He is trampling out the vintage where the grapes of wrath are stored... He hath loosed the fateful lightning of His terrible swift sword... His truth is marching on.*

Truth? Danny felt confused about God and what he'd seen of war. North and South, killing each other. Could there ever be a "Union" after this? Blacks fighting side by side with whites at Fort Wagner... while their families were being attacked back on the streets of New York. Then there were the Christians who helped slaves escape on the Underground Railroad, and Frederick Douglass's "Christian" master who wouldn't let him read the Bible. "Oh, Jesus!" he groaned. "Does any of it make sense?"

But while he let Regent graze on whatever tender blades he could find among the tough marsh grasses, Danny pored over James's Bible. There was a marker in the Psalms. Danny could guess why.

King David seemed to know a lot about trouble. He was always complaining to God about his enemies: *"My foes have trampled upon me all day long, For they are many who fight proudly against me."* Not just other kings, but sometimes his own people. And his own family! But to Danny's amazement, King David's trust in God never seemed to waver. *"When I am afraid, I will put my trust in Thee.... In God I have put my trust, I will not be afraid."*

But there wasn't much time for Bible reading when Danny and Regent finally arrived at the docks along the Sono River. The senior officer on duty read Captain Emilio's note and squinted at Danny. "You from the Fifty-Fourth?" Danny gulped and nodded, for the first time realizing the Fifty-Fourth was back *there* and he was *here*—alone.

But the officer stuck out his hand. "Heard your regiment fought like tigers against terrible odds at Fort Wagner. You can be proud."

When word got around the docks that the boy with the clubfoot was from the Fifty-Fourth Massachusetts Infantry and that he was taking Colonel Shaw's horse back to New York, soldiers on fatigue duty and sailors from the ships went out of their way to speak. "Good men, the Fifty-Fourth." "The Union army is lucky to have men like the Fifty-Fourth." "Sorry to hear about your colonel. We need more officers like him."

Brushing Regent's coat until it shone in the sun, Danny was starting to relish the praise when a couple of familiar voices brought him back to reality.

"Well, if it ain't our friend Turtle."

"Heard your regiment's been whittled down to size."

Danny closed his eyes and leaned his forehead against Regent's side. Tom and Sam. Why did he have to keep tripping over those two? *My foes have trampled upon me all the day long....* Well, *that* was the truth. But as he turned around and looked into the eyes of his tormentors, he realized... they were jealous. Jealous that his regiment had been part of the action while their regiment must have been left behind on fatigue duty.

On the spur of the moment, Danny decided to ignore their stupid comments and try a different tactic. "Hi, Tom. Hi, Sam. Good to see someone from back home."

Tom and Sam stared at him.

"I know you appreciate a good horse, Tom," Danny continued. "What do you think of Colonel Shaw's horse?"

Tom seemed confused. But he seemed to notice Regent for the first time. He nodded grudgingly. "Nice horse." He walked around Regent, running his hand over his smooth rump and sides and stopping by the horse's head. Regent nibbled on the buttons of Tom's blue jacket.

"Hey! Cut that out!" But Tom was laughing.

Sam just continued to stare back and forth between Tom and Danny. "So how'd you get the big job of returning the colonel's horse?" he challenged.

Danny shrugged. "Well, you know me—can't walk straight, can't run. So if I have a chance to ride a great horse like this one, you know I'm going to take it."

Bringing up his clubfoot first seemed to totally dismantle Tom and Sam's stock collection of taunts. "Well," Tom said gruffly, giving Regent another appreciative pat, "take care of this one. He's worth two of that ol' nag you used to ride back home." He grabbed Sam's arm. "C'mon, Sam. We got work to do."

Danny watched the two young privates walk away, then blew out a deep breath. Looked like there was more than one way to "stand up" to his enemies!

The trip by Union ship from South Carolina to New York took nearly a week, with stops in North Carolina and Virginia to pick up military mail and any wounded being shipped home.

Wandering the upper deck, Danny winced at the long rows of men with missing arms and legs or bandaged eyes.

Passing a group of off-duty sailors poring over a newspaper picked up in port, Danny thought he heard the name "Frederick Douglass." He edged in closer. "Could you read that part again?" he asked.

The sailor with the newspaper looked him up and down, then shrugged. "Can't say as I blame ya for wantin' to know. It affects your regiment—an' all the other colored regiments, too." The group parted to let Danny in. The newspaper rattled in the wind as the sailor read aloud.

Abolitionist Frederick Douglass, known for his pull-no-punches oratory, declared publicly last week that he would recruit no more black men for the Union army unless President Lincoln promised to protect them just as other prisoners of war are protected. "How many Fifty-Fourths must be cut to pieces, its mutilated prisoners killed, and its living sold into slavery, to be tortured to death by inches, before Mr. Lincoln shall say, 'Hold, enough!'"

Danny felt faint. What had happened to Sojourner Truth's grandson, who was still missing? Or Sergeant Simmons? He hadn't allowed himself to think about their fate if they had been captured. But now—

"Easy now," said one of the sailors, catching Danny as he wavered unsteadily. "That's not all. Douglass must have put some pressure on the president—listen to this."

Today President Abraham Lincoln issued a proclamation which states: "For every soldier of the United States killed in violation of the laws of war, a Rebel soldier shall be executed, and for every one enslaved by the enemy or sold into slavery, a Rebel soldier shall be placed at hard labor until the other shall be released and receive the treatment due a prisoner of war."

The Union sailors grunted. "Guess the president means business."

"Yeah, but look at this Virginia paper." A Confederate newspaper was produced, picked up at the last port. "Editor says, *'The very foundation of slavery would be fatally wounded if we were insane enough to treat black men as the equal of white, and insurgent slaves as equivalent to our brave white soldiers.'*" The reader looked up, disgust written on his face. "Guess they don't get it. Ain't gonna be no slavery if the Union wins this war."

Unsteadily, Danny made his way back to Regent's stall in the hold below deck. He didn't want prisoners executed—either side. Was it too late for James Caldwell? Robert Simmons? But at least if Lewis or Charles were captured from this point on...

He buried his face in Regent's silky mane. *Oh, God, you gotta help us. Don't think people wise enough or good enough by ourselves.*

Wearily, Danny slid off Regent's bare back at the gate of the modest house on the outskirts of New York. If his directions were correct, this was Annie Shaw's house.

But staring at the house, Danny suddenly felt frozen to the spot. Did Mrs. Shaw know her husband of only a few months was dead? What would he say? He suddenly felt terrified. This was a refined woman, after all. And he hadn't had a bath since... since he couldn't remember when! Was his face dirty? Did his clothes—

The front door opened and a balding middle-aged man stepped out, squinting questioningly at Danny. Except for the bald head and curly, light-colored beard, Danny was looking at an older version of Colonel Shaw.

The man stared a moment at Danny, then rushed to the gate. "Young man! Young man! You've brought Robert's horse home!" He turned and hollered back into the house, "Annie, come quick! It's Regent—he's come home!"

Before he knew it, Francis Shaw—the man was indeed Colonel Shaw's father—had brought Danny inside the house, and Annie Shaw, dressed in black, her dark wavy hair parted in the middle and caught up in a black net at the back of her neck, was serving him some iced tea and bread. He ate hungrily, hoping his manners weren't too bad. But he hadn't tasted any bread this good since he'd left the Douglasses' kitchen three months ago.

Mr. Shaw and his daughter-in-law plied Danny with questions. They had heard that Robert had been killed in the assault on Fort Wagner, but they didn't know any of the details. Danny was uncomfortable. He didn't want to describe how Colonel Shaw had died. But they wanted to know. Everything.

"Where... where is he buried?" Annie's voice was sweet and sad with her loss.

This was the worst of all. How could Danny tell this young widow that Colonel Shaw—a Union officer—had probably been stripped of his uniform and dumped in a ditch with his dead black soldiers as a humiliation. But she wanted to know. Everything.

When Danny got the words out, Mr. Shaw stood up and paced back and forth, fingering his beard

140

thoughtfully. Then he stopped in front of Annie and took her hand. "They meant it as dishonor. *But I consider it an honor* that my son is buried with the men who so valiantly fought to the death beside him. There he is buried and there he shall stay."

Thanks to the generosity of the Shaw family, who bought him a train ticket to Rochester, Danny once more settled under the wing of the Douglass family until his uncle Thomas returned from his job as war correspondent. Neither Wendell nor William were anywhere near the classy horse that Regent was, but Danny was still glad to have a horse beneath him as fall began to nip the air along Lake Ontario and touch the leaves along St. Paul Road with tips of red and yellow.

Returning to the large, rambling house after doing stable chores the evening of September 7, Danny was met by Rose, who set a cup of hot chocolate on the table, then said with a sly wink, "I'd leave that hot chocolate waiting, if I were you, and go see what Mr. Douglass is reading in the study."

Curious, Danny made his way through the dining room and sitting room, then paused at the study door. Frederick Douglass looked up from the newspaper he was reading beside the fire. "Ah! There you are." Douglass handed over the newspaper with a twinkle.

Danny couldn't miss it. The front page headline read: *Fort Wagner Falls!* Heart pounding, he quickly skimmed through the accompanying report. "...bombarded by Union artillery from land and sea for six days... final assault came at 9 A.M. on September 6 at low tide..." Huh, Danny thought. The generals had learned *something* from the last assault, which had been attempted at high tide. He read on. Once more the Fifty-Fourth Massachusetts had lined up in their ranks to be among the first to storm the walls. But during the night, the defeated Rebel troops had crept away; the fort was deserted. Fifty-eight days after the first assault that had spilled the blood of so many of their fellow soldiers, the Fifty-Fourth stood victorious within Fort Wagner's walls. Fort Sumter would soon be back in Union hands—and Charleston was doomed.

Danny looked up. Frederick Douglass rose from his chair. "No doubt the information you were able to give them from inside Fort Wagner was a great help," he said soberly. "Oh, this came for you today." He reached into his breast pocket and handed Danny a letter.

Puzzled, Danny slit the envelope and pulled out a pretty sheet of paper. *Dear Danny,* the letter began, *The war is not yet over. But when, by God's grace, the Fifty-Fourth returns, they have every reason to stand tall, as men who have earned their country's respect. And when they march once more through Boston, it would give me great pleasure if you would lead Regent at the head of the regiment, in memory of my dear fallen husband.* The letter was signed, *Annie Shaw.*

He read it again. Lead Regent? At the head of the

regiment? Even with his awkward hop-step, hop-step, which she had very well seen with her own eyes? Danny gaped at Mr. Douglass. "She said—"

Mr. Douglass smiled. "I know." He laid a firm hand on Danny's shoulder. "You stand tall today, young man."

More About Frederick Douglass

WHO COULD KNOW THAT A SLAVE BABY BOY, born at Holme Hill Farm in Talbot County on the eastern shore of Maryland in February 1818, to Harriet Bailey, a slave, and a white father (possibly Aaron Anthony, the white overseer), would grow up to be one of the nineteenth century's most eloquent orators and one of its most famous abolitionists?

Frederick Augustus Washington Bailey, sent to his master's brother in Baltimore at age eight to be a companion for two-year-old Tommy Auld, was taught to read by Tommy's mother—until her husband forbade it. After all, black people who learned to read "got ideas," and it "ruined" them for slavery.

Exactly.

Frederick had a passion for learning and taught

himself—and then taught others. After a conversion experience at age thirteen, Frederick soaked up Christian teaching from an elderly black mentor, Charles Lawson, and joined the Bethel African Methodist Episcopal Church in Baltimore. Sent back to his owner, Thomas Auld, at age fifteen, he conducted a secret Sunday school for other slaves, using the Holy Bible to teach them to read—until the Sunday school for blacks was busted by Thomas Auld (a Sunday school teacher himself) and several other church men.

For his impertinent spirit, Frederick was sent to work for a year for Edward Covey, a "Negro breaker." No matter how hard Frederick tried, he got whipped for anything and everything that went wrong. Finally he fought back—not to injure Covey, but to keep from being injured. Standing up for himself made him "feel like a man" and kindled a deep desire for liberty.

Frederick finally managed to escape from slavery September 3, 1838, at age twenty. His sweetheart, a free black woman named Anna Murray, joined him shortly and they were married on September 15 in New York, aided by the New York Vigilance Committee. At this time, Frederick changed his last name to Douglass (after a Scottish lord in Walter Scott's epic poem, *The Lady of the Lake*) to disguise his identity. The newlyweds settled in New Bedford, Massachusetts, which had an active cadre of abolitionists.

Frederick was only twenty-one when he made his

first public speech, denouncing proposals to colonize freed slaves in Africa and demanding that they be treated as free and equal U.S. citizens. Abolitionists sat up and took notice. In August 1841, he was invited to speak at the Massachusetts Anti-Slavery Convention, where he spoke eloquently about his life as a slave. Within a few years he was considered a major spokesperson for the abolition movement—speaking, writing for abolitionist newspapers (and eventually starting his own, first the *North Star*, which later became *Frederick Douglass's Paper*), and writing the first of three autobiographies. His speaking tours took him overseas to England where he was received with great interest and respect.

In 1848, Frederick and Anna Douglass settled in Rochester, New York, to raise their growing family of two girls and three boys. Anna, who was illiterate in spite of Frederick's attempts to teach her to read, took in sewing to supplement Frederick's speaking fees. The Rochester home sheltered slaves escaping to Canada, as well as a gathering place for local children who enjoyed an evening being entertained by Frederick singing and playing his violin.

The abolitionist movement did not speak with one voice, and eventually Douglass split with William Lloyd Garrison and Wendell Phillips over Garrison's "disunion doctrine" and whether the Constitution was pro-slavery. (Douglass took the position that the Constitution, properly interpreted, was *not* pro-slavery, and the United States should remain united and *all* its citizens free—nothing less.) Abolitionist John Brown tried to talk Douglass into supporting his plans to arm slaves and spark an armed rebellion. Douglass admired Brown's goals and his passion, but refused to support the ill-advised raid on Harper's Ferry on October 16, 1859—but because of his friendship with Brown, an order for Douglass's arrest went out. Douglass slipped out of the country on an already scheduled speaking tour in Europe—during which his ten-year-old daughter, Annie, died.

In 1861, Frederick Douglas supported the newly formed Republican Party and its candidate, Abraham Lincoln, as the nation's best hope to end slavery totally. He was at times impatient with and critical of Lincoln's "slow steps" toward total abolition and full equality, but in this plain man from Illinois—who said: "This Union could not long endure half slave and half free; that they must be all one or the other, and that the public mind could find no resting place but in the belief in the ultimate extinction of slavery"—Douglass found "the proper standard bearer... against the slave power."

Lincoln was elected the sixteenth president of the United States in November 1860; on December 20, South Carolina made good on its threat to secede from the Union if he was elected. At first the federal government made all sorts of concessions to appease the South (Secretary of State William Seward said, "Terminate however it might, the status of no class of people would be changed by the rebellion"—that is, slaves would still be slaves no matter who won the war). But the South would not be appeased.

Lincoln was inaugurated on March 4, 1861. Confederate artillery fired on Fort Sumter from Charleston, South Carolina, on April 12. The Civil War had begun.

Douglass welcomed the outbreak of the war. He had no hope that Southern slave owners would by reason and moral persuasion voluntarily give up the slave system. For two years he used his writing and oratory skills to plead for the right of blacks to fight and prove their loyalty to the Union and their worth as U.S. citizens. "The iron gate of our prison stands half open," Douglass said. "One gallant rush... will fling it wide."

The overwhelming losses suffered by both sides at Bull Run, Antietam, and Gettysburg made it clear: black troops were needed in this war. President Lincoln gave Massachusetts Governor John Andrews the go-ahead to raise two regiments of free blacks in the northern states (the only other black regiments to date had been made up of freed slaves in southern states, who mostly ended up on garrison duty to free white soldiers to fight). Andrews appointed abolitionist George Stearns of Boston to recruit; Stearns turned to Frederick Douglass. "Will you help?"

Two of Douglass's sons—Lewis, age twenty-two, and Charles, age eighteen—were among the first recruits from New York to volunteer for the Fifty-Fourth Massachusetts Infantry, commanded by Colonel Robert Gould Shaw, son of Francis Shaw, a deeply dedicated Boston abolitionist. The Fifty-

Fourth proved themselves worthy soldiers on James Island and at Fort Wagner, but Douglass met personally with President Lincoln on August 10, 1863, to discuss discriminatory practices such as unequal pay, unequal treatment of black prisoners of war, and difficulty in becoming officers. Both men developed a deep respect for each other, and after Lincoln's assassination, Mary Todd Lincoln sent Douglass the president's walking stick as a gift.

All of Frederick Douglass's sons returned home alive from the war. Douglass was elected president of the National Convention of Colored People in 1869; challenged President Andrew Johnson who waffled on equal rights for freed slaves; used his speaking and writing to support the Fifteenth Amendment giving black men the right to vote; was appointed U.S. Marshal of Washington, D.C., by President Rutherford Hayes; and later was named General Consul to Haiti by President Benjamin Harrison—to name just a few of his political efforts. For several years after the war, blacks made great strides in the area of civil rights and citizenship.

In 1882, Douglass suffered from grief and depression when Anna, his wife of forty-four years, died and was buried back in Rochester, New York. Two years later, however, he married Helen Pitts, a well-educated women's rights activist. The interracial marriage was criticized by some, but Frederick and Helen Douglass were invited to dine at the White House by President Grover Cleveland. The Douglasses shared many mutual concerns and enjoyed eleven years of companionship before Frederick died of heart failure in 1892.

In 1887, three hundred members of the Fifty-Fourth Massachusetts (including Lewis Douglass, who had returned to the South as a teacher after the war) held a reunion in Boston against a background of increasing racial violence after federal troops had been withdrawn from the South. They called on the U.S. Government to use "every proper means and influence it may possess to see to it that the colored defenders of its life in its day of peril, and their kindred or race, have the full and equal protection of the laws."[1]

By 1900, however, black voters had been successfully eliminated from the rolls of every Southern state by discriminatory voting regulations—an injustice that remained until the civil rights movement of the 1950s and 1960s.

---

[1] Clinton *Cox, Undying Glory—The Story of the Massachusetts 54th Regiment* (Scholastic, Inc., 1991) p. 152.

For Further Reading

Cox, Clinton. *Undying Glory—The Story of the Massachusetts 54th Regiment.* Scholastic, Inc., New York, 1991.

Burchard, Peter. *One Gallant Rush—Robert Gould Shaw & His Brave Black Regiment.* St. Martin's Press, New York, 1965.

Douglass, *Frederick. Douglass. Autobiographies: Narrative of the Life of an American Slave (1845); My Bondage and My Freedom (1855); Life and Times of Frederick Douglass (1881).* Literary Classics of the United States, Inc., New York, 1994.

Duncan, Russell. *Where Death and Glory Meet—Colonel Robert Gould Shaw and the 54th Massachusetts Infantry.* University of Georgia Press, Athens, Georgia, 1999.

Glory. A film starring Matthew Broderick, Denzel Washington, and Morgan Freeman about the Fifty-Fourth Massachusetts Infantry. Available on home video. "The heart-stopping story of the first black regiment to fight for the North in the Civil War." Rated R for graphic war scenes. (Also be aware that certain historical figures, such as Sergeant Major Lewis Douglass, are ignored in this version.)

Ritchie, Barbara, editor. *The Mind and Heart of Frederick Douglass: Excerpts from Speeches of the Great Negro Orator.* Ty Crowell Co., 1968.

CPSIA information can be obtained
at www.ICGtesting.com
Printed in the USA
LVOW07s1735111217
559405LV00005B/1294/P